FROM FLORENCE WITH LOVE

Allie, a young teacher, answers an advertisement for a helper at a school in Italy. But when she flies to Florence there is an incident with a strange man. Meanwhile, difficulties pile up after Rod, who runs the school, discovers how weak Allie is at speaking the language, and then she faces problems with the police. While sightseeing in Florence, she sees the mystery man again and knows she must contact Rod for help.

Books by Sheila Benton
in the Linford Romance Library:

MOUNTAIN LOVE
AN AUSTRIAN AFFAIR
CHATEAU OF THE WINDMILL
WHISPERS FROM THE PAST
FALLING LEAVES

SHEILA BENTON

FROM FLORENCE WITH LOVE

Complete and Unabridged

LINFORD
Leicester

First published in Great Britain in 2011

First Linford Edition
published 2012

British Library CIP Data

Benton, Sheila.
   From Florence with love. - -
   (Linford romance library)
   1. Love stories.
   2. Large type books.
   I. Title II. Series
   823.9′2–dc23

   ISBN 978–1–4448–1106–3

Published by
F. A. Thorpe (Publishing)
Anstey, Leicestershire

Set by Words & Graphics Ltd.
Anstey, Leicestershire
Printed and bound in Great Britain by
T. J. International Ltd., Padstow, Cornwall

This book is printed on acid-free paper

1

Allie's voice was high with excitement but tinged with uncertainty. 'I've done it, Jan. I've given in my notice.'

Jan stared at her young flatmate and gasped. 'Say that again. Are you quite serious?'

'Yes,' Allie continued more soberly. 'I'm really serious. In fact. I'm surprised I've lasted there as long as I have.'

Jan's round face was full of concern. 'What are you going to do? Are you sure you're doing the right thing, or have you got something lined up that I don't know about?'

'Absolutely not. You know I would have told you if I had. It's the car,' moaned Allie. 'It's broken down again. The headmaster said I'm a bad example to the children as I'm continually late.' She raised her eyebrows. 'He's right, of course. I agree with everything he says — but I can't afford a better car and that's all there is to it.'

Jan frowned. The problems with Allie's little car were well known — in fact, it was a joke between their friends. But this was serious. The school was several miles away and public transport was practically non-existent.

'So what are you going to do for money?'

Allie knew Jan was probably thinking about her contribution to the tiny flat they shared. She couldn't blame her friend for thinking that way, because even with them both working, they had trouble meeting the bills.

'Don't worry. I've had to give a term's notice and that gives me plenty of time to find something else. I think I should have done it long ago — or not started there in the first place, and saved myself this continual worry about transport.' She hesitated, then went on bravely, 'Perhaps I'll find something better.' It was said with confidence

— but if she allowed herself to think, the prospect of another job in just a couple of months was not that promising.

'Oh you'll find something,' said her friend, in a voice she would use for consoling a child.

Allie suddenly brightened. 'Perhaps I should aim for a complete change,' she said slowly, nodding and causing her dark shoulder-length hair to swing from side to side. 'That's what I'll do! I'll make a career change. After all, people do it all the time now, even older people — and at least I'm young.'

'Well, you won't find it easy,' said Jan dubiously. 'You've only ever taught — and you haven't even been doing that for very long. What on earth could you do, Allie?'

'Oh — something, preferably more exciting. Ideally I'd like to travel. It would be nice if I could use my Italian. It's coming on well.'

'Nice to know that all those evening classes you've been doing haven't been wasted then.' Jan teased. 'I thought you were just learning it for when you managed to save enough for a holiday in Italy.'

Allie quickly changed the subject, knowing she hadn't always worked as hard as she could at her classes. 'Shall we forget about it all and go out tonight? I've got a whole term to find something, and that'll be quite long enough.' Behind her back she crossed her fingers because, in spite of her flippant announcement, she was worried.

* * *

As the weeks flew past with only a couple of unsuccessful interviews, Allie started to panic. There weren't many jobs around, and Jan was right — she was inexperienced in anything except for teaching small children. She started to watch the pennies, fearing that she would soon be without any income at all.

The two local agencies, which she had thought might solve her problem, had nothing satisfactory. Anything she considered remotely suitable tended to be in an area without good public transport links, and she felt she simply couldn't cope with the worry of another job where she had to rely on her decrepit old car.

'Maybe I'd better move to another part of the country,' she said without enthusiasm. 'But what I fancy is working abroad for a couple of years.'

'I think that would suit you,' her friend agreed.

'I've never had the opportunity to travel very much.' Allie pulled a face. 'Or the money.' She turned impulsively to Jan. 'Do you fancy coming with me? Let's have a sort of late gap year.'

Jan shook her head in horror. 'Sorry — but It's not something I'd like to do. I'm settled where I am.'

Finding employment became Allie's main topic of conversation and she knew she must be driving everyone crazy continually talking about it. Her mother worried about her and kept telephoning.

'You must come home, dear,' she said. 'You know your father and I would love to have you back here, and there's always your old room — it's just as you left it.'

'Thanks, Mum — that's nice to know, but I do want to stay independent,' she said, swallowing the sudden lump in her throat.

Jan was a tower of strength, organising their social life to keep her mind occupied and listening to her talk, sometimes late into the night. But although she tried to think positive that something would turn up, her spirits soon dropped to zero.

The end of term loomed, and by now Allie even felt it was an unjustifiable expense buying the papers — so she took advantage of reading them in the library in an effort to cut down her costs further.

It was there that she saw the

advertisement for an assistant to help in a small, family-run language school in Italy just outside Florence.

The word *Italy* seemed to jump from the paper and, studying the listing carefully, Allie grinned. It was made for her! It fitted the bill perfectly. Her confidence lifted as she read the small print. An assistant with knowledge of Italian was needed to help the main teachers, both in class and with course work. Teaching experience was required, and there would be some administration work. Her spirits started to lift even higher, and she realised suddenly how tense she'd become with the worry of job hunting.

Italy! She'd once started saving to go there — but if she got a job in the country, that would be brilliant. Spreading the paper out smoothly on the table, she read and analysed every single word. Her heart lurched. Had she the courage to work in a different country, leaving all her friends and family behind? *Stupid,* she told herself firmly. Italy was quite near — nothing to worry about at all. She simply had to take advantage of this opportunity.

Every word of the advertisement was copied out carefully — avoiding paying ten pence for a photocopy — and, once home, she tried to convince herself she should apply for the job. After all, she was an experienced teacher, which also meant she did quite a lot of administration work. She was learning Italian. There was no point in hesitating and before she knew what she was doing, her hand had reached for the telephone and punched out the number.

Swallowing with a suddenly dry throat, she listened to the ringing tone. Then it was answered and it was too late to back out.

The conversation went well — much better, in fact, than Allie had dared to expect. It transpired that the preference was for a younger candidate, and she had teaching experience and a knowledge of Italian. The voice on the other end of the line had sounded middle-aged and almost motherly, so she had begun to relax and explain how interested she was in the job and how much she would love to go to Italy. Before she knew it, an interview had duly been arranged.

* * *

When Jan arrived home that evening from her office job, Allie was staring into space with an idiotic grin on her face. Her slim body was slouched in a chair and she had a large bar of chocolate in her hand.

'I've found the perfect job,' she said, brandishing the chocolate bar and then hugging herself with excitement.

'What kind of job?' asked Jan cautiously.

'My kind of job.' She sprang up, grabbed her friend and twirled her around. Quickly she filled in the details, and told her about the interview. 'What do you think, Jan? Doesn't it sound brilliant?'

'Err — well, I can understand you being so excited, and of course it sounds ideal for a teacher.' Jan looked at Allie seriously. 'I hate to say this, but just how good is your Italian? I don't want to put the damper on it, but honestly — what is the main language spoken at the school?'

Allie's face fell. 'Well, it could be better. It could actually be a lot better; I just hope that as the students are learning English, the idea will be that they practise it during the day. But, Jan — they want to meet me. I'm getting the train to London next week and if I suit, I'll be off to Italy pretty soon. Can you believe it? Think of the sun, the pasta — and all those lovely Italian men.' She rolled her eyes upwards.

'I can see it has its attractions,' Jan said slowly. 'But are you sure you'll like working abroad? And do you really know enough Italian?'

'Oh, don't be so *cautious*. I feel the job is made for me. It's just what I want, and a complete change.'

Her smile left her for a moment. 'Of course I'll hate leaving you and everyone — and I'll have to revise and listen to my language tapes like mad for the next few weeks — but I'm sure I'll get on okay.' Then her face clouded again. 'And of course I'll have to survive the meeting.' She started to pace the room. 'What shall I wear? What shall I aim for? Should I look very English, or try to look Italian?'

Jan grabbed her shoulders. 'Neither — just be yourself. Really, with your dark eyes and hair you might be taken for an Italian anyway. Of course, I think the women are usually plumper than you, but you could pass perfectly well.' She grinned. 'They'll love you.' she added generously.

★   ★   ★

On the day, Allie chose a smart skirt and top and to make herself look more efficient, fastened her hair on top of her head. Then adding gold hoops to her ears, she slid on some high heels, told herself to think positive and caught the train for London.

The interview was to take place in a hotel, which she found easily enough for it was large and imposing. Walking into the lobby, she felt out of her league and her knees began to shake as she was overcome with nerves. What was she doing here, pretending that her Italian was good enough to live in the country? An Italian speaker would probably interview her and if that happened, she knew she was lost. Her steps faltered as she considered turning tail and going home.

Then common sense took over — after all, she'd paid good money for the train fare. She had to go through with it, or it would be a waste of money which she could ill afford. There would also be the problem of explaining both to Jan and her parents as to why she'd backed out.

The young, beautifully turned-out

woman at the reception desk seemed to know all about her and she was shown to a small room off the main lobby. Here, to her surprise, a middle-aged couple greeted her, and she recognised the woman's voice from her phone call.

Quickly she glanced around the room searching for someone else. Perhaps another person would join them. She looked towards the door, but it appeared there was just the three of them in the room. This didn't seem at all like she expected.

'Take a seat, my dear,' the man said and gallantly pulled up a chair for her. 'Would you like coffee?'

Allie thought quickly. Coffee would be very welcome, but it could cause complications — she might end up spilling it or slopping it in a saucer and spoiling the impression she was trying to give.

'No, no, thank you very much. I was early and stopped for one on the way.' She hoped she'd be forgiven for the lie.

'Well, we might as well begin.'

The woman did most of the talking while the man sat poised with a pen and pad. They were involved with the school, although they were based in Britain and didn't actually live there.

'It's useful to have someone here to deal with the prospective students, and we're part of a team that interviews both students and helpers. It isn't often that we have to take on new staff.' They explained that there was no one leaving, but due to expansion the school needed another person to help in the day-to-day running.

Allie was asked a few simple questions about her teaching. 'What age group do you teach? Have you ever taught older students?'

'I know I've only taught young children — ' this was the part that worried her — 'but I'm sure I'd adapt to older pupils.'

They assured her that she'd find it easy as there were very mixed ages at the school, although obviously no young children.

'Now,' the woman said, 'you tell us about yourself and ask any questions and we'll do our best to answer you.'

Allie enquired about the situation of the school, the size and whether the students were encouraged to speak English at most times.

'English is recommended as it aids the learning process, but obviously you'll need a knowledge of Italian.' The woman hesitated. 'Is there a problem? You said you'd learned the language. Unfortunately our colleague who is an Italian speaker isn't able to be here today, so we can't give you any form of test.'

Allie's heart sank, as she knew she would have to bluff her way through it. 'Well,' she said brightly, 'I must admit I haven't got a language qualification but I've been studying it and am sure I can manage.' She'd have to work hard at it before she travelled to Italy, if they gave her the job. She couldn't let this lovely couple down.

'I take it you are reliable.' It was more

of a statement than a question and she nodded in agreement and tried not to think of the problems with her car and her lateness at school. It was all surprisingly low-key.

Now most of the questions were over, she relaxed. Having expected a brisk businessperson to interview her, it had been a surprise to find this pleasant couple. They were easy to get on with, more like two extra parents, and certainly there was no cause for alarm. She sensed that they liked her immediately, and she responded to their warmth. It was so incredibly simple that it went almost too smoothly, she thought. There didn't even seem to be anyone else in the running for an interview.

The man looked up from his notepad and the woman nodded to him. 'We'll confirm it in writing of course, my dear,' he said, 'but I think you can take it that the job is yours. If you want it, of course,' he said with a pronounced twinkle in his eye.

★ ★ ★

Later that evening Jan again found her friend sitting in a chair, chocolate in hand and smiling to herself. 'How did it go?' she asked. 'But looking at you I can probably guess . . . '

'It's mine if I want it.' Allie sprang up, whirled from the room and returned just as swiftly with two glasses and a bottle of wine. 'Oh, Jan — they were lovely people. I won't be working with them, of course, they just do the interviewing over here.'

'What were they like?'

'We-ell . . . ' Allie spun the word out slowly. 'They were an older couple who seemed impressed with my teaching experience. The money isn't brilliant but I get free bed and board at the school. And best of all — ' she couldn't keep still and clutched her friend in a big hug. 'Best of all, I get to explore Florence on my days off! Some of the villages surrounding it are worth a look too.'

'It's definite, then?'

'Yes, I've already phoned Mum and Dad. I know they'd rather I stayed here, but they were happy for me and promised to take a holiday there so they can check I'm okay.'

Jan smiled at her friend's enthusiasm. 'Well, I hate to lose you. But,' she raised her glass, 'here's to Florence.'

'To Florence,' Allie echoed seriously. Then she laughed. 'And a crash course in Italian for the next few weeks.'

'What about the language? Did they give you a test or anything?'

Allie gurgled with laughter. 'I was so lucky. Evidently there was supposed to be a third person interviewing but she couldn't get there — and guess what, she was the Italian speaker.' She grinned widely. 'So after all that worrying you did, I wasn't asked to speak. They sort of took my word for it.'

Then she had the grace to look a little shamefaced. 'But I'm going to work really hard in the time left before I go. In fact,' she said dramatically, 'I've a bit of cash put away and I'm going to have some private lessons just to top up the evening classes. There, what do you think of that?'

'I think you've been extremely lucky,' Jan said slowly. 'I just wish I had your ability not to worry about things.'

Allie looked lovingly at her friend. Dear, loyal, sensible Jan; she would hate to leave her and the flat. She'd been such a good friend. Her more serious nature toned down Allie's exuberant personality.

'I told you it would be all right, but I will work hard. Then I must buy something extra smart to travel in. The first impression I make at the school will be really important.'

'I've got a bit of news, too,' Jan said. 'Someone I work with has had to leave her flat and is willing to share with me here.'

'Oh, I'm so glad. I was really worried about leaving you with all the expense.' She grinned. 'I was even trying to work out how I could give you a couple of weeks rent to tide you over.'

'Well, you won't have to now. But any time you want to come back, I'm sure we could squeeze you in for a bit.'

Allie swallowed hard. It was just the sort of generous thing that her friend would say, and for a moment she regretted her decision to leave and try for a job abroad. But there was nothing here for her to stay for; no job, nor any prospect of one, and not even a current boyfriend. It would be difficult to leave her family, Jan, and her other friends but although it was another country and culture, she was optimistic that she'd soon settle and they could come and see her for their holidays. She tried to stop her thoughts running away with her, knowing she must keep her feet on the ground.

After all the excitement it was difficult to sleep. Allie lay awake for a long time while she replayed all that had happened in the last few hours. Then she tucked the events of the day firmly into a special corner in her mind so that she could take them out and relive them at any time. She was absolutely content — and if that nice couple were anything to go by, her future employers would be easy to get on with too. In fact, they would probably look after her and make sure she was happy in her job.

Her last waking thought was *Florence, here I come.*

2

A few weeks later Allie was on her way to Florence Airport. Bubbling with anticipation, she couldn't concentrate on her paperback, but passed the time looking round at her fellow passengers and wondering why they were travelling. Although she'd hoped to strike up a conversation with someone, it hadn't happened, which made her realise she was very much alone. At least it had been a smooth journey, and for that she was thankful.

It had been difficult at first to keep her nerves at bay through the flight. However, by taking deep breaths and telling herself she was on a wonderful adventure, she had at last managed to relax. After the pressure of trying to get to school and coping with the problem of her car, she decided she deserved this job. A little voice kept asking her if she was really sufficiently qualified, but, being Allie, she pushed it to the back of her mind.

Suddenly there was the excitement of landing, and a buzz of anticipation filled the plane as passengers reached up to retrieve items from overhead lockers. People were trying to squeeze past each other as though it was a competition to see who could leave the plane first.

Making her way to the airport bus, she gazed around. This airport looked just the same as the one she'd left a couple of hours ago, if much smaller — but there was a totally different atmosphere. For one thing, it was a lot warmer. Shouldering her hand luggage, she climbed aboard.

It was standing room only, and she took the opportunity to glance down at her outfit with a satisfied smile. Jan had lectured her on making a good first impression at the school. 'You must aim for slightly understated but smart — yes, definitely smart. We'll go out and choose something really nice for you to travel in.'

'Thanks, Jan,' she murmured under her breath as her stylish navy cotton trouser suit drew several admiring glances. She flicked back her hair with pride and excitement.

Once through the airport checks, she trudged along with the crowd making for the exit and taxi ranks. It was hard to believe that she was actually here at last, and everything felt simply wonderful. What an amazing time it had been — going to the interview, getting the job, and now it was all really happening.

Shuffling along with the crowd, she transferred her bag from one shoulder to the other. As she did so, her lower arm brushed against the pocket of her suit. Something was different. She was sure there had been nothing in any of the pockets; she had not wanted to spoil the smooth line of the jacket by putting anything in them. Her step hesitated; yes, there was a bulge in the right-hand one. Feeling the outside with her fingers, she was sure there was now a small object in it.

How very strange. Had Jan popped something in as she left? No, she was positive nothing like that had happened. Frowning at the oddness of the situation, she stopped. Just as her hand was about to slip into the pocket, she felt a heavy push on her back and nearly stumbled. A pair of hands gripped her shoulders almost painfully, but at least she was upright. Turning to thank her rescuer, she gasped. Instead of a gorgeous Italian man, this one was swarthy-skinned and sinister-looking. She managed a strangled 'thank you', forgetting that she was supposed to be speaking Italian. The figure grunted and spun away from her, but seemed to brush hard against her as he turned. As she watched him disappear into the crowd she checked to see if she had got all her luggage — and realised her pocket was now empty.

What an odd thing to have happened!

But the object, whatever it was, had certainly gone. There was nothing she could do, as she'd no idea what it had been — if, perhaps, it had ever existed. Maybe it was just her imagination. If so, then it wasn't worth bothering about. Shrugging, she put the whole thing out of her mind.

Once outside, it was as though she was in a different world. Rapid Italian was interspersed with tentative English words as people asked where they could find transport. Revelling in the atmosphere, she couldn't stop smiling, thinking of all the places she could see in her time off.

She was so busy people-watching and listening to fragments of conversation that, when she looked at her watch, it struck her that she'd been standing there more than fifteen minutes in her world of daydreams. Taxis came and went, picking up people who looked so sure of themselves, and in contrast she began to feel like a small lost child.

The plane had been on time, and she

was in the right place. Then it hit home that the person meeting her was late. But she willed herself not to panic; after all, anyone could be late for any number of reasons. She started to list them in her head. Puncture; couldn't get away from the school; traffic problems — there were no end of excuses for lateness. After all, she should know; she was the expert.

As she glanced around, she noticed a man who seemed vaguely familiar. Then it registered that he was her rescuer — or, she suddenly thought, maybe he was the one who had pushed her!

'Stop it, Allie,' she mumbled to herself. 'Get a grip.' She shook her head, trying to clear the odd thoughts away. However, part of her mind had already noticed that he was dressed all in black with large sunglasses. A suspicious-looking figure if ever there was one.

The thought whirled around in her head that surely he wasn't connected with the school, as she didn't fancy getting into a car with him. Then it dawned on her that he'd been on her flight — but she'd barely registered him at that time. He'd been just another passenger.

Without being obvious, she tried to watch him. Before long, fortunately, he walked swiftly away and she saw him drive away on a scooter.

'Thank goodness he's gone,' she mumbled again and then realised she'd been muttering to herself several times since arriving.

Standing there trembling, she was suddenly aware that she was cold and a little frightened. The longer she waited, the worse she felt as her confidence drained away. She'd obviously been mad to come all this way on her own without knowing a soul.

Surely someone must come for her soon — but thank goodness it wasn't that sinister-looking creature. Well, all she could do was wait. There was an address for the school, but she had no idea how to physically reach it. If the worst came to the worst, she supposed she could just give the address to a taxi driver and hope for the best.

★ ★ ★

Suddenly a car came roaring towards her, then slowed abruptly to a stop. Allie stepped back involuntarily, not wishing to be associated with such a maniac of a driver, but the window opened and a voice called, 'Allie Holt.'

'That's me,' she answered tentatively.

'Come on, then. I'm in a rush.'

'Are you meant to be meeting me? How do I know who you are?' she replied cautiously.

'I'm Rod Darwin from the language school and I'm supposed to be meeting you. Isn't that enough? After all, I know your name.'

Because he made her feel silly and unimportant and she'd had a stressful time, she looked at her watch and, completely out of character, snapped,

'Well, you're extremely late.'

The driver's door opened and a man in T-shirt and casual trousers strode towards her. In no time her case was lifted and she was propelled in an undignified manner to the passenger side. The door was swung open and she was told, 'Get in.'

'I thought Italians liked women and treated them well,' she said in a thoroughly bad humour, knowing she was suffering from reaction after the episode with the man but unable to do anything about it.

In a moment he sank onto the seat beside her. 'But I'm not Italian. Can't you work that out? It is a language school you're going to, you know.'

'I don't actually start until tomorrow, so don't try testing me today because I'm not employed.' She gasped at her own audacity and wondered if at the end of the day she would have a job at all. She was determined to make her point, but at the same time hated herself for being so rude to this complete stranger who after all, had come to pick her up.

'Anyway,' she queried, 'why were you late? I was beginning to worry. A girl doesn't like to hang around airports on her own, especially foreign ones. At least,' she attempted a laugh, 'this one doesn't.'

He glanced across at her. 'I'm sure you'd have managed. Someone would have come to your rescue.'

'That's no way to treat the staff.' She was starting to feel thoroughly bad-tempered at his lack of concern. 'At the school I've been working at, well, they wouldn't treat any one like that.'

'Maybe you shouldn't have left,' he answered and lapsed into silence.

I should have kept my mouth shut, she told herself bitterly. *He must have hated coming to meet me when he was so obviously busy.*

She wondered briefly if she should tell him about the strange man she'd seen at the airport, and the object that was in her pocket and then wasn't. No

31

— it didn't make sense. The whole episode had been, to say the least, peculiar. Her breath caught in her throat now she had time to think about it and she gasped aloud, remembering the horrid-looking man. To think that his hands had actually been on her shoulders! But surely she was making too much of it; after all nothing had happened.

Hearing her exclamation, Rod turned, saying, 'Are you okay?'

'Oh — yes,' she said, forcing her voice to sound casual. Then the moment was gone — the moment when she could have told him.

Determinedly she worked on calming herself until at last she was relaxed enough in the passenger seat to study her companion. Early thirties, she thought. Not exactly good-looking, his face was too strong for that, but definitely attractive with dark eyes and hair that waved slightly. She'd noticed his height when they'd first met, and his hands on the wheel were tanned and long-fingered.

'What do you do at the school?' she ventured after a time. Allie was not a girl who enjoyed long silences, preferring to chat companionably to anyone she was with. 'I expect you teach,' she said, answering her own question.

'I run it,' he said briefly.

'Run what?' She could hear the gasp again in her voice.

'The school. What else?' He turned towards her, repeating it as though to a child. 'I run the school.'

'Oh!' Suddenly she felt that it was all going to be beyond her. Everything had happened too quickly. Leaving her flat — the flight — no one to meet her — and now this man with the offhand manner was her boss. Added to which she was suddenly on the verge of tears.

Biting her lip, she said, 'Oh,' again in a small voice and turned away to stare out of the window.

He glanced swiftly across at her, 'I'm sorry. I'm not usually so rude. It's not your fault but I've had a hell of a day.'

'It's okay. I'm not usually so rude, either.' They turned and grinned at each other. Then she realised that they were driving slowly along the side of the river Arno, and over the dark water she could see a succession of bridges. 'Oh,' she breathed, her tears forgotten. Is that the Pont Vecchio?' She gazed at the distinctive arches and the small shops perched on it. 'It looks fascinating! Can we — ?'

'Not today, I'm afraid. The school is just outside Florence so you'll be able to come in on your days off.' He added, 'Believe me, I know what it's like when you first see Florence, but you'll have plenty of time.'

No offer to bring me, she thought a little petulantly.

Peering from the window she noticed a row of scooters parked and many others ridden by young people. *Do all the youngsters ride scooters here?* she wondered, and thought suddenly of the odd man at the airport. He had driven off on a scooter. She looked anxiously around, hoping that he'd left Florence and she wouldn't see him again. Maybe she should have mentioned the incident to Rod after all — but it was too late now. Besides he was still talking to her.

'There's plenty to see,' he continued. 'The galleries, gardens and of course the Cathedral.'

As they started to leave the city behind them, she twisted round to look back, knowing she would want to visit it time and time again.

'I suppose you'd like to stop for a moment,' he said almost grudgingly and slowed down.

She twisted round in her seat to face him. 'Oh — could we, just for a moment? I'd like to look at the river properly.'

'Tell you what, we'll stop for a coffee. I expect you could do with one and I know I certainly could. I'm late anyway, so I suppose a few minutes more won't make much difference.'

He swung the car into a space on the opposite side of the road to the river with practised ease. They got out and, sensing her eagerness, he grabbed her arm. 'I'll take you across the road.'

'I'm not a child. I'm capable of crossing the road, you know!' Allie, infuriated, tried to shake him off.

'You're new to this place; you might even look the wrong way when you step off the pavement.' He hustled her quickly across in a gap in the traffic. 'Just a quick look at the river, mind you, and then an even quicker coffee. I really must get back.'

'It's not a very good colour,' she remarked, leaning on the wall and looking down at the water. 'I hate to say this but I'm a bit disappointed. It's looking very dark — I expected it to be beautiful.'

'No, it does look a bit muddy,' Rod admitted. 'But when it's evening there is often a lovely light that makes it look golden, and of course the bridges are beautiful and well worth exploring.'

By the softening of his voice and the expression in his eyes, she knew that he was a man who loved this city.

Suddenly she realised they were leaning on the wall looking down at the river like any romantic tourist couple. She turned to him, but his gaze was fixed firmly on the water.

Then the spell was broken. Briskly he took her arm once more, but she was reluctant to move.

'I've longed to come to Italy — and especially to Florence,' she breathed. 'Can't we stay a little longer? And I'd love to cross the Pont Vecchio. I've heard it's full of jewellery shops.'

'Yes.' He grinned and looked almost carefree. 'But not in your price range or mine, I fear.' His grip on her arm tightened. 'Sorry to spoil things. I really must get back, but we'll get that coffee and sit outside so I can point out to you where the main attractions are.'

Maybe he wasn't so bad after all — and the poor man had obviously had a very bad day. He'd looked extremely tense when they'd met.

Rod found two seats outside a cafe

and in no time at all there was a fragrant, steaming cup of coffee in front of her. She sipped it, savouring the special continental aroma and flavour, and considered the man opposite her. Maybe she'd misjudged him. Now, sitting drinking coffee together while he told her a little about Florence, he seemed a different person.

In between pointing out places she should visit, she was aware that he was also studying her. She was glad that Jan had talked her into buying the smart trouser suit, and that she'd had her hair trimmed before she came.

As she sipped the drink, she was aware of that little bubble of excitement again, and she now looked forward to arriving at the school. The incident at the airport was pushed firmly into the back of her mind.

At last, with a brief, 'Time we got going,' he got up to lead the way back to the car. Craning around, she caught tantalising glimpses of busy squares where, amid the bustle, people stood chatting and the drift of water from a dozen fountains caught the sun. She vowed she would return to explore as soon as she possibly could.

3

The hills around Florence were now heavy with mist. With the motion of the car Allie began to feel drowsy and relaxed. It had been a long day, full of small events that she began to turn over in her mind.

There was the strange episode of the man at the airport, which bothered her at the time but didn't seem so important now. At least Rod seemed quite human, and not the monster she'd thought when they had first met.

Actually, she acknowledged, he could be charming — and was certainly good-looking enough to be interesting. Yes, she would probably end up liking him, and was sure they would get on well in the future. There couldn't possibly be anything wrong with a man who loved Florence so much.

The object of her thoughts broke her

pleasant dream. 'I shouldn't have let you talk me into stopping for that coffee.' He glanced quickly at his watch. 'I'm now going to be really late back, which will put my schedule right out. I've lost the morning dealing with other business and it's going to be one heck of a problem catching up today.'

Allie caught her breath with indignation. 'I did not talk you into stopping for coffee. That was your idea.' She turned more fully in her seat, wishing she could see his face, but he was concentrating on the road. 'I thought it was a friendly gesture on your part, but I see now that I was totally wrong. I don't think you've got a welcoming bone in your body!'

She must have imagined or misinterpreted the moment of warmth they'd shared earlier in the café, because it evidently hadn't affected him.

If she thought he was annoyed enough to reply and continue the argument, she was disappointed. His only response was a explosive 'Huh!'

Allie glanced once more at the strong face beside her and lapsed into silence, deliberately closing her eyes. Outwardly she appeared calm but behind closed lids she was seething. She was, she reasoned, young, female and in a foreign country, and about to start a new job. So it was reasonable that Rod should make an attempt to put her at her ease. But no. He seemed completely without feeling. But a warning voice in her head told her to be careful and learn to keep her thoughts to herself — because, after all, he was her boss. She didn't intend to come all this way to get dismissed on the first day — and the way she was carrying on, it could easily happen.

The journey continued in silence. Had she offended him? Maybe he was one of those men who didn't like talking and driving. But that wasn't her style. She was interested in everything around her and liked to chat as well.

Oh well, she thought, *let's plunge in and try again and if he doesn't like it, well, that's just too bad.*

'Can you tell me something about the school?'

He glanced sideways at her and said abruptly, 'What do you want to know? Wasn't everything explained at your interview?'

She turned back to study him, feeling both rejected and dejected. There was no trace of a smile on his tanned face. Surely it wouldn't be too much for him to tell her something about where they were going?

However Allie was not a girl to be intimidated. 'Obviously — but you must appreciate that now I'm actually here, it's different. Asking about a place in another country is one thing, but being there is quite another.'

'Ask what you like — but I warn you, I'm not in a patient mood.'

'I had noticed,' she said, trying to imitate his abrupt manner. Then, more gently, 'Are you always like this or have you just had a really awful day?'

'You could say that.' His manner

certainly left a lot to be desired.

She resolved to make one more overture of friendship and said quietly, 'Would you like to talk about it? I always find it helps.'

He was silent for a moment and she thought that was all he was going to say. But then he spoke. 'I'm really sorry. I know I've not been too welcoming but the police have been at the school today.'

'The *police*?' Allie licked her suddenly dry lips and her voice rose. This was not a good start. The fact that she was in a foreign country made her feel insecure, and she began to regret taking the job.

'What for?' she asked, and then wondered if she really wanted to know. Hopefully it was just some minor offence to do with one of the students.

'Nothing that need concern you, but it's better you know they were there because someone is bound to tell you.'

'But I take it everything is all right? You aren't harbouring dangerous criminals there, or anything?' She attempted a joke. 'They didn't tell me about that at the interview.'

Obviously jokes weren't his thing because he answered seriously. 'Mainly they were just checking on something, so hopefully this will be the end of it.'

Allie was silent for a time, wondering what had been going on at the school. She tried to relax once more. It was obviously nothing to do with her. He said she had nothing to worry about; she must hang on to that thought.

She may eventually have dozed, because when she opened her eyes it was to find they were slowing down and running along a curved drive edged with the silver foliage of olive trees. As they reached the end, a building with a flight of steps loomed large. She gulped; this place was impressive to say the least, and she found it quite intimidating.

And then the sun came out and shone on the facade, lighting up the windows, and immediately it turned into a fairy castle.

'You know the school was once a hotel?' He broke into her thoughts.

'Yes,' she answered.

'Most of the hotel features have been left, so it is very comfortable.'

That was something; she felt she could definitely do with some comfort, and not just the physical kind. But it would have to wait for the moment. An acute ache of loneliness rushed through her like a physical pain, as she realised there was no one in this country she could turn to for comfort.

Rod swung her cases out of the boot. She followed him up the steps and through the doors into the entrance hall. Her steps halted for a moment as she took in the enormous proportions of the place. The floor was polished marble and cool to her feet. Her mood began to lighten. The school was truly a lovely place.

Rod spoke abruptly. 'I'll show you your room and then later I'll introduce you to the rest of the staff.'

'Okay,' she said brightly, determined

not to let his manner get her down.

Following him up the wide staircase, she would like to have looked down at all the splendour, but she scuttled after him like a puppy. Something told her that he now wanted to get rid of her as soon as possible and she had better not keep him waiting.

He opened her door. Following him in, she noticed the ceiling was high and the whole room light and airy. Net curtains blew in the breeze and dark shutters stood on each side of the windows. The bed was huge enough for three people. She giggled to herself at the thought.

'See you later, then.' He dumped her bags and made to leave, but turned back at the door to say, 'I hope you like the room.'

She was so surprised at his change of attitude that she responded wholeheartedly. 'It's really beautiful, thank you.'

Then she was suddenly alone.

How could anyone be anything but happy in such lovely surroundings?

Allie did a little dance and then flopped down on to the pale terracotta throw, gazing rapturously around at the light blue walls. It was so spacious! She tried to imagine how many times her room at home would fit into it. Shafts of light from the moving net curtains cast shadows on a large, dark wardrobe. It was a romantic and feminine place with a wonderful Mediterranean colour combination. Her last thought before her weary eyes closed was that Rod had left her in the room without making any arragements to show her around — or at least let her know where she'd be working.

★　★　★

It seemed much later that a knock at her door roused her. Crawling reluctantly from the bed, Allie opened the door to be confronted by a dark Italian woman dressed in a white shirt and trousers. She seemed to be in her early thirties, an attractive woman with large dark eyes that were full of self-assurance and experience. Allie immediately felt very ordinary and young, without any of the obvious sophistication of the other girl.

'I'm Christina. Rod asked me to show you around the school.'

'Oh — thank you.' Then, conscious of her ruffled hair, she mumbled, 'Please excuse me for a moment while I tidy up. I'm afraid I fell asleep.' She glanced at her watch; she had only slept for about half an hour. 'You know how it is with travelling — suddenly it all catches up with you.'

She knew she was babbling and smiled in what she hoped was a friendly fashion, but the woman did not appear to appreciate it. Allie instinctively knew that here was someone who would never arrive anywhere sleepy with messed-up hair.

'Where is the bathroom?' She tried a tentative smile.

Christina raised her elegant eyebrows and opened what Allie had thought was a cupboard door. 'We all have our own bathrooms because the building was previously a hotel.' Her voice was low, her English near-perfect with just a slight trace of an accent.

'How I hate beautiful, clever women,' she muttered to herself as she slipped inside the bathroom to rinse her hands and face and tidy her hair. She barely registered the pretty decor in the well-equipped room, and her stomach lurched as she wondered if she would be able to cope with the job. There was something about the immaculately dressed woman that was intimidating. Would all the staff be like her? Wouldn't there be anyone of her own type to pal up with while she was here?

'So what do you do?' she ventured as they walked side by side down the wide staircase.

'I run the art department,' the woman replied briefly.

'Oh — I thought the school was only for language.'

'The art department is new. Something of a venture for Rod and myself.' There was something about the way in which she said his name that made Allie look up. There was a subtle inference in the statement that Christina and Rod were an item.

She nodded. She couldn't say that Christina was unpleasant, exactly — but certainly not over-friendly.

There were so many rooms and corridors that Allie was soon completely lost. Then they came to a room with a huge dresser, which reached nearly to the ceiling and took up almost the entire end of the room.

'Here we take our meals, which are very good. Rod likes his food.' Again that inference of intimacy. But why? Perhaps she was being warned off. *As if that were necessary!* thought Allie and quickly suppressed a giggle.

She walked up to the dresser. 'The hotel must have been built around this!' She attempted a light-hearted remark.

'I don't think so,' responded Christina quite seriously. Then, abruptly, 'I'm sorry, I do not have the time to show you outside.'

'That's all right, I'm happy to wander around alone.'

'I'll leave you, then.' The woman seemed to positively glide away.

Having met two people, neither of them particularly friendly, Allie was quite relieved to step out and breathe in the fresh air on her own for a while. Immediately she found herself in a courtyard with a fountain playing in the centre. Beyond it, she could see a terrace of lemon trees, and beyond that the hills. The mist hung above them like a cloud of small feathers.

It's a magic place, she thought. *I can live with this luxury even if the people aren't really my sort.* But she couldn't help hoping that among the staff there would be a kindred spirit — someone to go out with, and sit chatting with at mealtimes.

Leaning over the fountain, she ran

her hands through the moving water, feeling the coolness on her wrists, totally unaware that she was not alone. A young man watched her, admiring the fall of dark hair and the grace of her slim body and arms as she tried to catch the droplets of water.

'Hello! You must be the new girl.' The voice was English without any accent. Allie straightened up quickly to meet the eyes of a young man of about her own age. *Definitely not Italian*, was her first thought as she took in his fresh complexion, fair hair and blue eyes.

Suddenly things seemed to be looking up, because his expression was warm and friendly.

'I'm Allie and I've just arrived. I think I'm going to be a general helper.'

'Jamie.' He held out his hand. 'We knew you were coming, of course. How are you settling in?'

'Things have been . . . well, a little difficult.' She decided not to go into details. 'But my room is lovely, and the whole place is beautiful. What exactly do you do here?'

'Oh, very ordinary. I teach English. Have you met anyone yet?'

'Only Christina,' she said quietly.

His eyes twinkled. 'Oh — the lovely Christina. Quite a lady, that one. Not a woman to cross, I might add, so stay on the right side of her.'

Smiling back, Allie knew she was going to like Jamie. He seemed her type of person — smiling, easy to talk to, and above all, friendly.

'I've also met Rod, of course — he came to pick me up at the airport.' She hesitated, aware that it might not be very wise to comment on her new boss, but suddenly she added impulsively, 'He's not the friendliest of people either, is he?'

Jamie looked surprised. 'He's quite a good guy, usually — but I expect he told you the police were here this morning.'

'Yes, he did mention it.' She grinned. 'So what happened? Did one of the students rob a bank?'

'Nothing so simple. They questioned everyone without telling us very much but Rod hinted it was something to do with importing stolen goods.'

'Stolen goods?' She was shocked. 'What happened? Was it a mistake?'

'No one knows — except Rod, of course. They just drove off, and he isn't saying much. It shook him badly because he's very protective of the school.'

Allie was silent for a moment and then decided to change the subject, as she didn't want to think about something like that going on at the school.

'Are Rod and Christina an item?' she ventured.

'Not really. She makes no secret that she would like that, but he's very careful where the staff are concerned.' He grinned down at her. 'Why, do you like him yourself?'

'Certainly not! We've only just met, and I think he's one of the rudest men I've ever come across.'

But even as she spoke, Allie knew she

was blushing — because there was something about her new boss that attracted her.

Jamie laughed gently at her. 'I think Sarah is in her office. She's the school secretary. And you'll be working with her quite a bit of the time. Shall we go and say hello?'

She nodded, and he took her arm in a casual fashion as they went back into the building.

'It's so big,' she grumbled. 'I'm sure I'll get lost.'

'It's a bit daunting at first but you'll soon find your way around. I'll draw you a map if you like and give it to you at dinner.'

'That would be great.' Allie smiled gratefully at him.

★ ★ ★

They found Sarah in her office and introductions were swiftly made. The other girl was pretty, with light brown hair and lovely hazel eyes — and, like

Jamie, had an open, friendly manner.

'I'm so glad you've got here,' she told Allie. 'There's so much to do and we might need extra accommodation for the next intake of students. Maybe you could help with that? How's your Italian?'

It was the very worst thing she could have said. Allie bit her lip, knowing she couldn't bluff her way around the issue this time. The thought of meeting people or making phone calls in the language made her feel sick and shaky. She really shouldn't have come — she knew that for sure now. Soon everyone would know that she had a problem with the language. It couldn't be hidden much longer.

'Well,' she mumbled, 'I have to admit it's a bit rusty at the moment.'

To her amazement, Sarah simply laughed and said, 'Okay — I won't throw you in at the deep end just yet. I'll give you time to get used to us all. Won't take too long. It's a case of sink or swim here, I'm afraid.'

She glanced across at Jamie. 'You've no idea how much our Italian has improved since we've been here.'

Allies legs nearly gave out with relief. Perhaps she would cope after all — and thank goodness she'd brought her books and tapes with her. Every moment in her room, she would have to practise and practise until she could hold her own. But at least, for now, she'd survived.

4

As soon as possible, Allie made her escape. More worried than ever that she was here under false pretences, she fled back to her room. Fortunately her instinct took her back to the main hall and she managed to make her way from there without too much trouble. Her mind battled to find a way through the situation; suddenly she wanted to be on her own with time to think. As she rushed upstairs, her mind was working overtime. There was only one thing to do — and that was work, with a capital W.

Flinging off her elegant trouser suit and pulling a wrap from her case, she settled on the bed with her Italian books, tapes and tiny recorder. Breathing deeply, she tried to settle down. Somehow her language skills must quickly improve. The idea of telephoning to find student accommodation had sent her into a panic. She just wasn't up to the job, that was the trouble — and no amount of bluffing was going to get her out of this situation.

An hour flew past as she concentrated like never before. Her eyelids wanted to droop as the day's travelling caught up with her, but she fought against the urge and managed to stay awake.

A rap at the door interrupted her. Turning off the recorder, she opened it and was shocked to find Rod, casually leaning against the wall.

'Oh,' she said vaguely, trying to gather her thoughts.

'Have I woken you?' He looked amused and she felt his eyes on the neck of her wrap. 'I expect today will have been quite tiring, and you were obviously lying down.'

Pulling the wrap more firmly around her, she answered, 'No, no — I was busy . . . ' Quickly she searched her mind but couldn't think of anything sensible to say and continued, 'er . . . sorting out some stuff.' She really couldn't admit to having to study the language.

'I've come to take you down to dinner.' He still looked amused. 'Unless, of course, you'd rather sleep.'

'Dinner?' A quick glance at her watch surprised her. 'Oh — yes, quite suddenly I feel hungry. It's later than I thought.'

'It's staff only tonight and we make it a bit special. So if you're ready?' He grinned as he looked again at her wrap. 'I don't think that would be quite suitable, but . . . er . . . interesting, of course.'

Damn the man, he was starting to make her feel both young and stupid. She glanced down, unusually lost for something to say.

'Of course — I'll get changed at once.' Then immediately she wondered what to do. He had the knack of putting her at a disadvantage. Should she shut the door on him, or . . . ? No — surely he didn't expect to be invited in.

He solved the problem saying, 'I'll wait.'

Allie looked round. Was he intending to stay outside? Surely he wasn't going to wait in her room. She hovered uncertainly but his raised eyebrow threatened disapproval at the delay. She grabbed her trouser suit and vanished into the bathroom. He'd have to take the initiative of where to go.

Fortunately she'd arranged some make-up items on the ledge earlier and after a few minutes, was ready to go to dinner. The door to the corridor was now closed, so she presumed he was outside, and instinctively her shoulders relaxed. The problem had been solved, thank goodness.

But then a slight movement drew her eyes to her bed on the other side of the room. He was there. Her hand flew up to her face to stifle a gasp as — horror of horrors — she saw him looking at her workbooks and tapes.

Allie Holt, who could always bluff

her way through situations with cheek and good humour, stood like a schoolgirl waiting for the explosion.

She was not disappointed. The grin had been wiped from Rod's face and his brows were drawn together.

'Is *this* — ' he waved the book accusingly in the air — 'the standard of your knowledge of Italian?'

She now knew what people meant when they said they wanted to sink through the floor. But he was waiting for her to speak, to give him some sort of explanation.

'I . . . er . . . was just brushing up.' Goodness — what was that stutter she'd developed since she'd arrived here? What on earth was the matter with her?

'Brushing up? I imagined you were fairly fluent. Well, at least competent. I know this is a school, but I don't expect to teach the staff.'

His sarcastic tone was bad enough, but his expression was truly frightening, and she felt more alone than she'd ever felt in her whole life.

It was childish, she knew, but she didn't want to listen and had to clasp her hands in front of her to stop herself from putting them over her ears. He was in full flow, and she allowed the tirade to wash over her while trying to decide how to handle it.

Eventually he paused, and stupidly she said the first thing that came into her head. 'Well — I haven't heard you or anyone else speak any Italian since I've been here.' Allie glanced at him fearfully, convinced she'd be on the plane home tomorrow.

The dreadful man looked her straight in the face and broke into a torrent of rapid Italian, with a very good accent. It was so quick that she only managed to translate about one word in three, and quickly gave up altogether.

What could she say to defend herself and apologise for trying to deceive him? On the verge of tears at the shock of his verbal attack, she at last muttered, 'I'm sorry. Of course, I'll go, and hopefully you'll be able to get someone else quickly.'

'Why did you answer the advertisement?' he said bluntly. She heard a tinge of disappointment in his voice.

A huge sigh came from nowhere as she spoke. It was time for the truth.

'I gave in my notice because I had trouble with my car and it made me late for school. There wasn't any public transport and I couldn't afford a better car.' She swallowed, 'I'd always wanted to come to Italy and I'm learning the language and I thought . . . '

Her voice trailed off and she was even closer to tears. Then she gathered herself and went on firmly. 'I've been working hard with the tapes and I thought that being in the country I could brush up before — well, before I had to prove anything.'

She tried to look at him but quailed. 'I really intended to give the job my all. I'm keen to learn, and the idea of being here was just too tempting.'

Well, one part of her mind told her,

he won't be very impressed with the way you're babbling. Not exactly Miss Efficiency, are you?

Silence fell. She glanced up at her boss's face and to her amazement, she saw the expression in his eyes soften.

He said quietly, 'Quite a story. Okay, you can stay. I'm not happy about what you've done — although I suppose it shows you have initiative.'

Relief spread through her at his change of heart and her voice shook as the worry ebbed away. 'Oh — thank you. You won't regret it, I promise you.'

'Okay.' He looked faintly embarrassed at her words. 'But tomorrow we'll work out a programme, and I'll check on your progress each week.'

He grasped her shoulders and shook her gently. 'And you must really work hard — or frankly, young lady, I'll consider you've taken this job under false pretences.'

Allie had the grace to look ashamed, but inside her heart was singing. It was a reprieve — and now she need no longer hide the fact that she wasn't very competent in Italian, which took a great deal of strain from her.

Just wait until she phoned Jan to tell her that she'd been found out so quickly. Jan would immediately say, 'I told you so! How did you expect to get away with it?' But then, she'd be amazed to hear that Rod had been so good about it and that he'd given her another chance.

'Okay, enough said. Now we'll go down to dinner.' He was watching her as the thoughts ran round her head. 'Hey, wakey, wakey — you look as though you're in a daydream.'

Allie blinked rapidly and pulled herself together. As he opened the door for her, she turned and said cheekily, 'Grazie' — just the one word of Italian — and didn't turn to see his reaction but preceded him to the bottom of the stairs. When she risked a glance, she saw that his eyes were smiling and with a light step she followed him into the dining room.

As they entered together she relaxed, feeling that they'd reached an understanding. Now there was nothing to hide from this difficult man, and she could enjoy her first evening with the rest of the staff.

It was surprising how few people there were, although she'd been told at her interview that the school was small and specialised. There wouldn't be many people to know, but on the other hand they looked a pretty friendly bunch . . . with the exception of one.

As though reading her thoughts, he said, 'Not many staff, as you can see. We only have three classes, with a limited number of students in each one. But we are expanding, as you may know, with the new art department.'

He paused as his name was called. 'Ah — Christina. I was just going to introduce Allie to the others.' He turned back to Allie. 'You've already met Christina, I believe?'

'Oh yes,' she answered and met the stare of the other woman. 'We've met.'

At that moment Jamie joined them, and somehow Christina contrived to steer Rod away from them.

Allie grinned. 'I don't think she likes me. What have I done?'

Jamie took her arm. 'You're younger than she is, pretty, and you walked in with Rod looking as though you were on the best of terms.' He laughed and squeezed her hand. 'Believe me, that's quite enough to upset the lady. Just ignore it. Come and sit with me tonight and leave Christina and Rod to their own devices. Of course, you know Sarah, too.' He indicated the school secretary who'd just walked in and Allie exchanged smiles with her.

'Now meet Liz and Pete — they're two of the other tutors and a married couple.' He led her to the other side of the room where the couple he had pointed out sat chatting with a drink. Allie took to them at once. They were clearly the oldest in the group, probably in their late thirties or early forties.

While Pete chatted with Jamie, Liz said warmly, 'I expect you're eager to explore Florence. We were just the same when we first came, and we've a car here, so any time we can give you a lift into the city just let us know.'

Allie was warmed by the friendliness of the staff — except, of course, the condescending Christina — but the Italian woman seemed to be the odd one out. Allie put thoughts of her firmly from her mind, resolving not to let the woman worry her.

But underneath the smiles and greetings she noticed an air of unease. Liz put it into words just before they sat down to dinner.

'I hope Rod wasn't too late meeting you but, as no doubt he told you, we had the police here questioning us about stolen goods. Evidently they'd had a tip-off that something was to be brought in today.'

'That's really dreadful. Rod was a bit late and I was beginning to be nervous — especially when this man . . . ' The end of her sentence was lost in the announcement that the meal was ready. *I'm obviously not meant to tell anyone about that strange few minutes,* she thought, and shrugged away the thought of the odd stranger.

The food was set out on a large table with a choice of fish or pasta, and they helped themselves. Wine was on the table; Rod laughingly explained that it was merely to celebrate their first day back and they were not to expect it every night.

He then gave a little speech welcoming Allie who, not usually a girl to feel self-conscious, nevertheless felt herself colouring up. There was a moment of panic when she wondered if she should reply but, after the company raised their glasses to her, the conversation became general. The little speech by Rod had reminded her vaguely of a wedding reception, and she half-expected other people to get up and say their piece.

The dinner was excellent, the wine

superb and the room splendid — but hanging over the room was that undefinable atmosphere that she couldn't quite make out. It was probably the result of the visit from the police — and that was nothing to do with her. Overall it was a good evening and the slight undercurrent was not enough to spoil it.

Jamie was as good as his word and sat next to her. Soon they were chatting and laughing like old friends. Now and again she felt Rod's gaze on her and wondered if he thought she was being too frivolous and not taking her situation seriously enough. However when she caught his eye, she simply smiled casually across at him and turned back to her companion.

'Find out as soon as you can when you get time off,' Jamie said, 'and maybe we can go somewhere together and I can show you round.'

Allie looked at Sarah, who was deep in conversation with Liz, and wondered whether she and Jamie were an item. The last thing she wanted was to upset the other girl. She'd like to make a friend of her.

'Are you taking a group?' Jamie was asking.

'Oh no, not yet. I've got to settle in first.' Allie didn't want to admit to anyone else that she had problems speaking Italian, at least not until she knew them all better. But probably Jamie would find the whole thing amusing, as his sense of humour seemed in tune with her own.

Rod sought her out after the meal was finished and led her into his office. 'You seem to be in good spirits now — certainly good enough to spend the evening laughing with Jamie. Be careful; I don't want that sort of thing getting in the way of work.'

'Really?' Her eyes opened wide and her back stiffened. 'I find him easy to be with, and friendly. Okay, we were getting on well — but then I need a friend here.' She was on dangerous ground, but that should shut him up, surely. What was it about being in Italy that brought out the very worst in her? Rod was her boss, but she was entitled to some social life without him breathing down her neck.

'Be careful how you speak, young lady, or I shall put you in one of the classes with the students. How would you feel about that? From teacher to student in one easy lesson.'

He'd got the better of her again. She knew her face was glowing red.

'Surely you wouldn't do that to me! I would feel dreadful — after all I've come here to teach, and everyone knows that.' Then, looking at his face, she could see he was teasing her.

Folding his arms across his chest, he looked at her appraisingly and answered, 'Well, it's nothing less than you deserve, the way you've acted about this appointment.'

Was he serious now? She'd no idea — but if he wasn't, she didn't think much of his idea of humour.

Her chin snapped up. 'Perhaps I should go, after all. I've barely unpacked — I could leave first thing in the morning if someone would give me a lift.'

'Quite a little temper, haven't we?' He leaned back, looking relaxed. 'Okay, I won't do that, but watch your step and consider yourself on probation. Come and see me here tomorrow, immediately after breakfast, and we'll work out what you'll be doing. Sarah needs help with the administration and you might be able to do a bit of teaching with our more advanced groups where we make them speak English during the lessons.'

She'd behaved badly again, and must try to be more her usual pleasant self before she was really in trouble.

'Thank you,' she said quietly. 'I'd like to say how sorry I am again — for everything. I didn't think it through properly and I should have done.'

'Well, it's too late now, so I'll see you in the morning and work out a plan of campaign. Goodnight.' And with that she was dismissed.

★ ★ ★

Allie mused as she settled for the night that she was lucky not to have been at the school when the police had visited that morning. How on earth would she have coped with an interview and questions when her language was so shaky? What a dreadful start that would have been. What a fool she would have made of herself in front of everyone. To bluff her way through a situation like that would have been beyond even her imagination.

How great it would be to talk this over with Jan. Maybe she could ring her soon — at least she could send her a letter with all the news. How lucky she'd been that Rod had discovered her problem, because now she somehow knew that he would shield her from the others.

Jamie was lovely, and it was obvious she'd found a friend — and, from the way he looked at her, perhaps he'd become more than a friend. They certainly seemed to get on well, and if he wasn't already with Sarah, it could be an interesting term.

5

Allie expected the first night in Italy would make her restless, especially as her head was full of the events of the day, but surprisingly she slept well. Running through her mind were all the people she'd met. She and Sarah could become good friends, she felt, while Jamie would be fun and was quite possibly interested in her. Rod with his strong personality, so sure of himself, could easily turn any girl's head. *He's your employer, that's all*, she told herself, her mind trying to override her emotions telling her he was off limits. Particularly as he was involved with Christina.

Springing out of bed, she looked happily round the room, for this was to be her first complete day in Florence. Unsure what to wear, it suddenly dawned on her that she hadn't even unpacked properly. Flinging open her case, she quickly hung her things in the wardrobe. After consideration she chose a simple, full skirt in her favourite deep blue that, fortunately, was crease-resistant. It was teamed with a paler blue top and flat shoes. Looping up her hair, leaving a few dark tendrils around her face, she stepped back from the long mirror. Hum . . . smart but casual; hopefully just the right look.

Fastening small golden rings in her ears, she peered closer. Eyes sparkling with excitement looked back as she swept on mascara to make them look larger. Quite Italian-looking! She preened a little and then, grabbing her bag, hurried down to breakfast.

After a quick meal shared with Jamie and Sarah, she left the table where the other two were still deep in conversation. It was early, and her steps took her out onto the terrace where the air was cool and the early morning mist hung high over the steep terraces, putting the distant hills into soft focus.

Catching her breath at the beauty of the landscape, she stood entranced, knowing that she'd never want to go back indoors. How she wished she was an artist and could paint this wonderful landscape! Then, suddenly, she became aware of a warm hand resting lightly on her shoulder.

'Look at the cypress trees standing guard above here.'

Somehow she wasn't surprised to hear Rod's voice — he seemed so at home in his surroundings.

'It's so lovely, it makes me tremble,' she said softly.

'And I thought it was the effect of my touch.' There was laughter in his voice and she swung round to face him.

The man was human after all; in fact, there was a good chance he was flirting with her, for she could see the interest in his eyes. Well, that was a surprise! But again, she told herself he was her boss. There was no way she was going to let herself respond, however much she might secretly wish to, so she ducked out from under his arm.

'This is the Italy I dreamed about,' she murmured. 'The foothills of olive groves and the recession of the mountains. It's truly a picture postcard.'

'I'll take you to Lucca at the weekend,' he said suddenly. 'You'll love the quaintness of the walled city.'

Suddenly she bristled, for it was like a command. He hadn't even asked if she would like to go with him; just assumed, in his usual high-handed way, that she'd agree.

'It has an eleventh-century cathedral and is also the birthplace of Puccini, if you're interested in opera.'

Thinking swiftly, she decided she might as well go with him; at least it would be an opportunity to see the walled city.

'Thank you,' she said softly.

'It will be a good thing for you to see as much of the locality as possible. It'll give you an insight into the Italian way of life and help you when you come to teach.'

Ah — obviously her imagination had got the better of her. He wasn't eager for her company or interested in her at all — but just the standard of her work. Well, what did she expect? She wasn't here to find romance. And certainly not with him.

Then he abruptly changed the subject. 'I came to find you for a reason, so come back to my office.'

She followed him meekly, wondering what had happened to her normal confidence. There was something about this man, or perhaps this place, that took away her usual high spirits and optimism.

Once inside, he shut the door and immediately said, 'I've just had a phone call from the local police and they'd like to interview you.' It was said in a matter-of-fact tone of voice, but hearing the word police, Allie felt a total panic creep over her. All her irrational dread of foreign policemen came to the fore and she felt the blood rush to her face and then drain away, leaving her cold and shivery.

'Hey,' he said softly, reaching out to steady her. 'Don't look like that! It's just routine, but they do want to speak to you.'

'To me?' She gasped and clutched the back of a chair. 'What on earth for?' Her imagination spiralled away with her fears and she wondered how she'd cope in a foreign prison. Shaking her head before panic gained the upper hand, she made an effort to listen to Rod trying to calm her.

'Don't look so alarmed. I've already explained, it's just routine. They want to see any new arrivals.'

She wiped her damp hands on her skirt. Surely there must be more to it than he said. But of course, she'd done nothing wrong. There couldn't possibly be anything to worry about. She just couldn't understand what was happening here.

'Hey — don't panic!' He put a warm, reassuring hand on her shoulder. 'As I said, it's just a formality.'

'But the language!' Her voice rose. 'Will they speak English?' Then noticing that her hands were clenched, she tried to relax and take deep breaths. After all, she wasn't a criminal. Why was she behaving so stupidly?

'I'll be with you.' He spoke reassuringly as though to a pupil in a class.

'Thank you,' she said quietly, not knowing whether his presence would help or make her more nervous.

'Ten thirty, here, tomorrow morning, so don't be late.'

'Tomorrow? So soon?' She turned away, wanting to get out of the office and back to the sanctuary of her room.

'I haven't finished speaking to you yet. Come and sit down. Enough of worrying about tomorrow. We must look at your programme for today. Obviously I've had to make a few changes.' He picked up some papers on his desk. 'I've written out a plan for your first week.'

He was so businesslike that it crossed her mind the shared moment on the terrace had not been one of intimacy at all. It had merely been his way of trying to put her mind at ease in order to prepare her for the news about the police interview. She'd come here with such optimism, and things seemed to have gone from bad to worse in such a short time.

'Allie.' His voice brought her back to the present.

'Oh — sorry. Yes, I'm listening.'

'So I want you to work with Sarah this morning.' He paused, watching her reaction. 'I know she's got plenty of filing to get through — it's always the same at the beginning of term.'

'Filing!' She opened her mouth to object. She hadn't come all this way merely to do filing. What a boring morning! But realising he was gauging her response, she thought it better not to argue.

'Then, during the afternoon, I suggest that you sit in on one of the classes to get the feel of what we do here. Sarah will let you know which one. It'll be fairly informal as only a few students are due in this morning, but we like to occupy them immediately. We find it helps them to settle in.'

Well — at least the afternoon sounded more interesting. But Rod wasn't finished with her yet.

'Then the rest of the time before dinner, you'd better spend on your Italian. Tomorrow morning you can show me what stage you've reached.'

He had it all worked out, and there was no choice but to do as he said.

'That's all,' he was obviously dismissing her. 'Don't forget — I want you here tomorrow morning to see the police.'

Bleakly Allie made her way to Sarah's office. What a start! This was not what she'd imagined it would be like in Italy. The whole situation was just too depressing — especially the looming talk with the police and Rod's regimented plans for her day.

★ ★ ★

'Cheer up.' Sarah was grinning at her. 'I hear we're working together.'

Somehow she'd reached the reception office, and the other girl looked so pleased to see her that she immediately felt better.

The morning passed quickly and over a lunchtime sandwich in the courtyard, she told Sarah about her reasons for coming to Italy. 'Rod wants me to work on improving my Italian for the first couple of weeks.' She managed to gloss over her language problem with a bright smile and knew that Sarah hadn't realised quite what a disastrous situation she was in.

'No boyfriend at home, then?' Sarah was obviously settling down for a good getting-to-know-you chat.

'Not at the moment — how about you?'

'Er no, not really.' But Sarah's voice was low and her eyes dreamy.

'Oh, but I think you've got someone in mind — I'm definitely getting certain vibes,' Allie teased.

'Maybe,' the other girl admitted, flushing slightly. 'Anyway — there'll be plenty of choice this term with the students.' She giggled. 'Several seem about the right age, although Rod is very strict about forming attachments. He's a bit old-fashioned that way, says it's not good for work.'

'He's offered to take me to Lucca at the weekend, just so I can get the feel of the area,' Allie announced. 'He seems to think it will help me settle here and of course it's a wonderful opportunity for me to see — '

'Oh — hello, Christina,' Sarah interrupted, speaking over her shoulder. 'Are you coming out here for lunch? It's a lovely day.'

'Oh, I rarely eat more than a piece of fruit for lunch. I simply wanted to have a breath of fresh air.'

Allie turned towards the woman and immediately wished she hadn't. How long had Christina been standing there? She'd obviously overheard something that had infuriated her. Allie almost winced because the look directed at her was full of dislike. She'd definitely heard her telling Sarah that Rod was taking her out — and she didn't like it one little bit.

'She hates me,' she said dramatically when she and Sarah were alone again on the terrace. 'I've only just arrived, and already someone hates me. To tell the truth, I find her a bit scary. She seems so intense.'

'Oh — her!' Sarah was sympathetic. 'Don't worry, she hates anything female, especially where Rod is concerned.' She lowered her voice. 'Just between you and me, she's infatuated with Rod. You can see the way she looks at him and she's always manipulating situations to be with him.'

'Does he like her?' Allie couldn't help asking the question.

'Ah — I'm not totally sure. You've probably noticed, he doesn't show his feelings much. Though I must admit she's a very attractive lady — but so unfriendly it's unbelievable. So don't worry about her, 'cause she's exactly the same to everyone.'

'Everything is going wrong and it's only my first day.' Allie pulled a face. 'How much worse can it get by the end of term?'

Sarah laughed. 'Why — what else is bothering you apart from Lady Christina? And she's not worth bothering about.'

'The police want to speak to me.' Allie glanced round as she spoke as though worried someone might overhear.

Sarah smiled and answered gently, 'That doesn't mean a thing. If you'd arrived here earlier yesterday, they would have spoken to you then. We were all interviewed.'

'Really?' Ally began to brighten up. 'What questions did they ask?'

'Just how long we'd been here, where we came from, and whether we were out anywhere yesterday.' She lowered her voice. 'I heard a rumour that there were stolen goods expected on one of the flights.'

'But that's when I arrived!' The awful sensation of panic returned. 'Surely they don't think that I — '

'No, no — of course not, silly, it'll only be routine. They have to question everyone. It's procedure.'

Allie breathed a sigh of relief. She wasn't being singled out at all.

'Sorry, I'm just being paranoid.' She grinned. 'Which isn't like me at all.'

The lunch break, full of girlie gossip, soon had her feeling relaxed. By the time she had taken a seat at the back of the room to watch Pete with his students, she'd forgotten all about the police. There were just a handful of students in the class and Pete had their full attention. He was making the lesson so interesting that Allie wished he was teaching her Italian. Fancy having a teacher like him to bring the language alive, instead of having to rely on her books and tapes! And thinking about those same books and tapes she excused herself from the class and hastened back to her room.

★ ★ ★

Later, preparing for dinner, Allie decided she was satisfied with the day. Her own studying had gone so well that she'd taken the trouble to do some written exercises to show Rod next morning. There was also a neat list of phrases written out to help her with the police interview. She should be able to tell them in their own language the time the plane landed and when she left the UK. All in all, she was pleased with herself and looked forward to a relaxing evening meal.

Dinner was every bit as pleasant as she'd hoped, and she now felt quite at ease with the other tutors. Watching Sarah carefully, she tried to gauge whether she was showing more than a friendly interest in Jamie, but though there was pleasant banter between them, it didn't seem serious. So when Jamie asked her if she'd like to go to Florence with him at the weekend on his motorbike, she smiled at him and was just about to say yes when she remembered — she'd already agreed to go to Lucca with Rod.

Sarah spoke for her. 'She's going sightseeing with the boss himself!' She grinned. 'Not sure whether that can be classed as a good day out or not.'

Jamie narrowed his eyes as though he didn't approve. 'What day are you planning to go?'

'Actually I don't know.' Allie knew she was flushing, although there was no reason why the head of the school couldn't show a new employee around, she reasoned.

The situation was resolved for her, however. Just as they were leaving the table, Rod came up to her and said abruptly, 'Allie, I'm sorry — we'll have to postpone our visit to Lucca.'

'Oh!' was all she could think of saying.

'Yes, Christina has a few problems with her course and I'll need to help her sort it out during the weekend.'

'It's okay — don't worry about it.'

Her voice was soft as she tried not to show her disappointment. He nodded and walked away.

'Well, his loss is my gain,' declared Jamie. 'So how about Saturday? We'll leave here early and see how much of Florence we can take in.'

Forcing herself to smile brightly, Allie tried to concentrate on what he was saying. 'Yes, that'll be perfect. I'm so looking forward to seeing Florence and have a list of places I want to visit.'

'That's great! We'll see what we can do.'

It was certainly something to look forward to, but Allie couldn't help feeling that her first choice would have been to go with Rod to Lucca. They didn't get on all that well, but there was something about him that drew her.

On the other hand, a day out with the younger man would be fun and relaxing — just as long as Sarah was happy about it. But as she looked around for her new friend, she realised that she was already speaking to Liz and Pete and laughing at something Pete was saying. So it must be all right — because she wouldn't want to tread on Sarah's toes, or try to take someone she was interested in.

In the quietness of her room she sat for some time at the window, staring out into the darkness and listening to small night-time sounds. It had been a good day, really; there was still the ordeal of the police interview to face tomorrow, but after her chat with Sarah, even that didn't seem such a terrifying prospect. Then there was the trip to Florence with Jamie . . . and maybe Rod would take her to Lucca another time.

That night, her bedtime reading was not her language book but a guide to Florence. She especially wanted to see the Cathedral and the Uffizi Gallery. Now her dream was about to become true and she felt she simply couldn't wait for the weekend to arrive.

6

The next morning arrived all too quickly. Allie decided to present a sensible and workmanlike appearance for the police interview. Then, while she was pulling out a pair of black trousers, she suddenly changed her mind as her old high spirits rose. After all, weren't Italian men supposed to be susceptible to attractive women? Surely policemen would be just the same.

So, although her top and trousers were demure, she left her hair loose and took care with her make-up. While she was dressing, she thought again of Jan and wished she could talk the situation through with her. Her friend was so sensible and level-headed; she missed her easy companionship.

Fortunately Sarah knew she was nervous about the coming interview and had saved Allie a place beside her at breakfast. 'Don't worry too much. I told you before that we were all questioned the day you arrived.' She glanced quickly at her. 'Honestly, it's no big deal. Why are you making such a fuss?' She grinned. 'After all this is Italy — far more relaxed than back home. With luck you might attract one of those good-looking Latin policemen, and that would really make your day.'

'I just can't help feeling worried. I've never been interviewed by the police before. I don't know what to expect.'

'Just some questions; your name, nationality and how long you've been here. Well, in your case, when you arrived, and probably what you're doing at the school and why you decided to work here. Simple questions, really.' She gave her arm a gentle squeeze. 'Cheer up! It'll be okay, honestly, and we can laugh about it later. You're working with me again this morning.'

Allie smiled gratefully and tried to cheer up. What a good friend she'd found in Sarah. Nevertheless, the thought of endless questions made her nervous — and knowing Rod would be there somehow made it worse. But on the other hand she would probably need him to help her with the language. Oh, what an awful situation! She certainly hadn't bargained for anything like this when she'd arrived here full of enthusiasm.

Sarah gave her another nudge. 'Hey! It'll be okay.'

Smiling, Allie tried to concentrate on her croissant, but inside her stomach, butterflies were running races.

Making her way to Rod's office, she took deep breaths and concentrated on the cool marble of the floor to help with her composure.

Nearly there now. As she walked she quickly rehearsed what she was going to say — in Italian, of course. Fortunately no one saw her, or they might have wondered about her sanity as she muttered to herself.

Yes, she'd say good morning, tell

them she was English and exactly when she'd arrived here. That would do for a start. Maybe it would even impress Rod if she started off in the language. They would be simple sentences; nothing that would trip her up or cause her to become confused.

Hesitating at the door, she wondered whether to go straight in, or knock like an errant schoolgirl. Tossing her head, she decided to go straight in; after all, she wasn't a child, even though that awful man made her feel like one. A little voice whispered that he also made her feel very much like a woman, but she pushed the thought from her mind. Somehow she must discipline herself where thoughts of him were concerned.

Determinedly she grasped the door handle and entered the room. Rod was at his desk with a policeman and woman at his side.

'Ah — Allie.' His voice had an edge to it. 'I didn't hear you knock.'

She flushed; the man was so unpleasant that she didn't think it worth a reply. She strode up to the desk and gave the policeman the benefit of her brightest smile. He was young and she saw a flash of admiration in his eyes. Hopefully this might be easier than she'd thought.

Concentrating on her best accent, she said, 'Buon giorno.' Her voice rose and she tried not to gabble. 'Sono inglese. Sono qui . . .'

'Okay,' Rod interrupted. 'I'm sure they know you're English and I think they'd prefer to ask you questions. So sit down.' He actually pulled a chair forward for her and the moment she'd been dreading was here.

Of course, he'd had to reduce her to a nervous state with his abrupt comments! He always managed to put her at a disadvantage, and now, trembling as she was, she felt glad of the solid chair. She sat on her hands, in case they shook, and focussed her whole attention on the two officers. She couldn't help noticing how attractive they were, both dark with lovely smiles, and the woman had the most amazing dark eyes with long lashes.

The man questioned her while his companion took notes. Putting her at ease with a smile, he spoke slowly and clearly. Rod must have primed them about her lack of language skills, because he watched her carefully as he spoke to make sure she understood. As she relaxed, a small miracle happened and she realised that she understood enough of the conversation to give brief and simple answers without asking for help. It was a good feeling, and her confidence grew as she sensed the approval of them all. As the interview progressed, it became almost like a friendly chat. Although Rod had eased back slightly, he was listening intently and she knew he was on hand to help her out if necessary.

He saw her out at the end of the interview and said very quietly, 'Well done. I'm quite proud of you.'

Just a few little words, but she looked up at him and saw his smile and knew that she was beaming in return. His praise was uplifting as well as being unexpected. It gave her a great feeling and as she returned to Sarah's office, it was as though she was floating on his approval.

★ ★ ★

It was later in the day when the thought hit Allie that she should have mentioned the odd-looking man on the motorbike to the police. Her heart dropped, for she knew she must tell Rod, and guessed he wouldn't be pleased that she'd forgotten the episode.

This time she knocked at his door. There was his smile again — but this time it was impossible for her to respond. Nervously she licked her lips.

'I just wondered if I should have told the police that there was a rather odd-looking man around when I was waiting for you.'

'A man?' His brows drew together in a frown.

'Yes — a strange-looking man. Well, I say strange, but there was something sort of scary about him that stayed in my mind.'

He scowled at her, which made her decide to play for sympathy — or at least appeal to his chivalrous nature. That is, if he had one.

'To tell the truth, he frightened me.'

A flash of something crossed his face — something that gave the impression that he cared a little.

It gave her confidence and quickly, before her nerve went, she told him all about the strange encounter that wasn't really an encounter at all. It sounded stupid, talking about the way she felt something in her pocket that had then disappeared.

'Why didn't you tell me about this at the time?' The disapproving scowl was back with a vengeance. And was it her imagination, or did he suddenly look taller? He certainly was intimidating.

'I tried to, but you were late and in a hurry and somehow — well, I just didn't.' She licked her lips nervously. 'Looking at it objectively, there's nothing to tell — but as I said, he scared me.'

Rod sat and stared at her. It dawned on Allie that he hadn't even asked her to sit down, but had left her standing facing him across his desk.

'You know the police will have to be informed.'

'Yes.' She was beginning to feel like a criminal, just because she forgot to tell him what happened. He had that effect on her.

'Let's get it written down,' he said suddenly. 'You tell me in English and I'll translate and see the police have it.'

Then he pulled a chair up for her and for the next few minutes they sat close together while they worked. She was aware of his body warming the space between them, almost as though he was gently touching her.

I can't afford these feelings, she told herself sternly. *Romantic ideas about him are off limits*. But glancing at the strength of his face, she somehow knew he could be relied on to help her through this situation.

He obviously had no such feelings about her, telling her quite bluntly that she had not only been stupid, but would cause the police some problems.

'That's the gist of it down. Now we'll go through it again and fill in the detail.' This time she became exhausted with all his questions. 'Give me a full description. How tall was he?'

'Er . . . ' Already she could sense that things were no longer so clear in her mind. 'Well, taller than me — but not as tall as you.' She saw the exasperated expression on his face. 'Medium height.'

'Can you describe this man? Was he young or old? You say he looked at you. What nationality do you think he was? What was he wearing — and the motorbike, what make was it?'

Trying to harness her thoughts she closed her eyes, hoping to remember her encounter with the strange man.

'He wore dark colours and sunglasses, and something on his head.' She felt close to tears. 'He frightened me. I just wanted him to go away. I tried not to look at him too much.'

She fell silent for a moment. 'I thought afterwards that he could have been the one who pushed me, although it seemed at first he was helping me. Really, it all happened so quickly — and there were lots of people.'

What about his eyes and hair? Or anything else?'

'He had sunglasses on but later, when I was waiting for you, I saw him again and I got the impression he was sinister-looking.'

'Don't be dramatic.' He sounded exasperated. 'And the bike? You said you saw him with a motorbike. What sort was it?'

'Honestly, I can't tell one motorbike from another, but it was small.'

'Could you pick him out if necessary in an identity parade?'

She licked her lips and the colour left

her face. Looking down at her hands she was surprised to see her fists were clenched. She didn't remember clenching them. 'Identity parade?' She swallowed. 'Oh, Rod, I do hope that it doesn't come to that. I don't think I can cope.'

He patted her hand and his voice was gentle again. 'It's all right. I'm just asking you all these questions so that, with luck, the police might not want to see you again.' He looked down at his writing, then looked at her and said, 'Do you think he would recognise you again?'

She blinked, startled for a moment at the abruptness of his question.

'Depends on how many strange women he looks at,' she said flippantly, but something told her that he wasn't amused. 'I suppose he would — after all, I wasn't hiding behind dark glasses or wearing a hat.'

That seemed to satisfy him and she thought no more about the question.

'Of course, it could be that this man

isn't involved in anything. It might have been quite an ordinary situation and general confusion while you were both making for the exit.'

'Yes, of course.' Her face cleared. 'Maybe we don't need to tell them at all! As you say it could be nothing, so why waste their time?'

'Of course you must tell them.' Did he actually sit up straighter so that he could glare down at her? The atmosphere changed abruptly and his moment of sympathy had gone. His expression was now hard, and she suddenly felt as though her face had been splashed with cold water.

'You should have told them in the first place. Don't you realise this puts you in a bad light? They were quite happy with your statement this morning — but now, well . . . ' He hesitated. 'You'd better sign this and I'll see it's taken to the police.' He pushed the handwritten paper across to her. 'I still can't understand why you didn't mention it to me when I picked you up.'

'You were late and I forgot — and really there didn't seem anything to tell.'

'I couldn't help being late, you know that — and obviously now I wish more than ever that I'd been on time. However, you should have told me about it then. If the man is part of the problem, it's probably too late to do anything about him now.'

His writing was strong and sloping, the hand of a confident person. Gazing at it, she had the strangest feeling that now she'd let him down.

'I'm sorry,' she whispered. 'But I was quite alarmed after having been waiting so long, and then when you arrived I was relieved to see someone and it went out of my mind.'

If she expected understanding, she was disappointed.

'It was ridiculous and inefficient. What sort of person are you? You must have heard the rumours about what's going on here and know the worry I have about the school. You could have mentioned this straight away.'

There was no point in arguing any more. No point in telling him that she didn't know anything was wrong when she first met him. He was determined to believe the worst of her.

Getting up quickly, her chair scraped the floor loudly, causing him to wince. This man was impossible! All her warm feelings towards him evaporated. She had to assert herself, or he would always get the better of her. Gathering up her courage, she retorted, 'I don't know whether I should sign this. How do I know what you've written? It all looks very complicated and there are a lot of words I don't understand.'

He stood up quickly. 'You silly girl, I'm trying to help you. Perhaps I should just run you to the police station and leave you there to sort it out on your own.' He hesitated and she wished she hadn't made the remark because he looked frighteningly angry. 'As you don't trust me, I suggest you spend the evening translating what I've written.'

He thrust the sheet at her. 'I expect this paper signed, and a written translation in English, on my desk first thing in the morning.'

She grabbed the paper and hurried out of the room on shaky legs. It was obviously not a good idea to provoke Rod. Halfway between tears and anger, she muttered to herself, 'It's almost like having detention!' She made her way to Sarah's office, stuffing the paperwork into her bag as she walked.

* * *

It was a relief to see Sarah and tell her about the whole encounter, and somehow discussing everything put it into proportion. Over coffee, she decided to confide in Sarah the whole sorry tale of applying for the job without good language qualifications.

It was such a relief when Sarah dissolved into laughter. 'This is the funniest thing I've heard for ages.' Then she hesitated. 'How did you get away with it at the interview? I was given a test by a very efficient woman.'

'The couple admitted that they were short of another person during the interview, and they were so sweet, but I really did wonder who they were. I expect they were standing in for someone.'

'I think they may have been friends of Rod's parents who stand in at short notice. I've heard of them before, but not met them.' Then she giggled. 'I don't expect he's very pleased with them now. But don't worry. It's not the end of the world and if you want to practise speaking, I'll help you. We can disappear into either of our rooms and do some work.'

Allie touched the other girl's arm, quite overcome with the generous offer. For a moment, speech was beyond her. Then, in the intimate mood of the moment, she managed to ask the question that had been bothering her.

'Sarah — are you and Jamie together, if you know what I mean?'

Sarah blushed slightly. 'At the risk of sounding corny, we're just good friends — very good friends. So if you're bothered about going to Florence with him, don't worry.' Then she grinned. 'I know you're not interested in him, anyway — you've got your sights set on our elusive Rod, haven't you?'

Blushing even deeper than Sarah, Allie answered more sharply than she intended. 'We don't get on. I'm definitely not interested! He's just my boss.'

Sarah rolled her eyes. 'Watch out for Christina!' She lowered her voice and said in a stage whisper, 'You have been warned.'

The rest of the day passed in a hectic whirl and Allie managed to push her worries to the back of her mind for most of it.

Working her way through Rod's handwriting after dinner, she mentally called him all sorts of names and had imaginary conversations where she got the better of him. But at last she completed the translation and fell into bed mentally exhausted.

Fortunately, the next day he was too busy to speak to her. With relief, she left her work on his desk when he was out of the office.

How she hoped that would be the end of it all, because at the moment she was tempted to go straight home. But of course, Jan now had someone else in the flat — and she didn't want to explain all this to her parents who would worry terribly about her. No; she'd just have to stick it out and hope everything would eventually turn out all right.

The only good thing was that she found she was picking up Italian quite nicely now. Although the staff spoke English to each other, she sat in a class and listened most afternoons, and it was surprising how quickly her mind was being trained. *With luck I shall leave here fluent*, she told herself.

There was the trip to Florence with Jamie to look forward to — and although she had been disappointed when Rod cancelled their arrangement, she realised how awkward it would be to spend a day with him at the moment. They were hardly on speaking terms.

7

The days until Saturday passed quickly, for the school was settling down and Allie was becoming used to her routine. No one showed surprise at the way her days were spent, assuming that Rod was helping her become adjusted to the new job.

So far she'd told only Sarah about her problems, both with the language and the odd man on the motorbike. They'd agreed that it would be a secret between them, and now someone else knew, Allie was more relaxed and less constantly on her guard.

Sarah told her not to worry about Rod, saying that he was a sweetie really with a bark worse than his bite. But she reserved her judgment on that. 'Sweetie' was hardly a word she would use for the domineering man with moods like night and day.

She was looking forward to going out with Jamie. He was fun and easy going and, knowing he and Sarah were just good friends, she could enjoy his company without fear of upsetting her new friend.

Saturday, when it came, was cooler than previous days but just right for sight-seeing. Allie dressed casually in cotton trousers and tee shirt as Jamie had a motor scooter.

He drove carefully, and they were soon leaving his scooter amongst many others in the town. As they parked, she realised that when she described the odd man as riding a motorbike, he was really on a scooter.

Looking along the lengthy row of two-wheelers, she thought with a shudder that he could even be here in the city.

'You must see the Cathedral first — or the Duomo, as they call it!' Taking her hand, Jamie led her through the crowds. She gasped aloud at the huge marble building that took up most of the square. Trying to stand back to get a better view, she reached for her camera. She'd known that Florence was beautiful but nothing had prepared her for her first view of the Duomo.

Jamie laughed as she twisted her camera first one way and then another. 'You won't get it all in,' he said. 'It's so large. Another day we'll go up to the dome because the views are fabulous, but today I'll just give you a taste of what there is to see.'

'It's magnificent,' she breathed. 'But what a crowd there is!'

'I'm afraid it's always busy, but perhaps more so today. Let's grab a coffee and you can sit outside and stare at all the grandeur while you drink. Then we'll decide where to go next.'

'If I could just see where everything is, I could come back another day and take my time,' she suggested.

'Okay — we'll have a look at the Uffizi Gallery next, but I bet there will be a queue there too. If it isn't too bad, we could go in.'

Only a few people were in line to buy tickets, however, and while they waited Jamie told her about some of the great paintings that hung there. 'We must get a guide. That way, you'll enjoy them even more when you know something about them.'

Once they were inside, Allie was completely lost in another world. 'I feel It's a privilege to be here,' she whispered.

'Everyone feels like that on their first visit.'

Drifting in and out of the display halls, they stopped to look through a window, which gave them a good view of the River Arno and the succession of bridges that spanned it.

Then Jamie turned and said, 'Hey look who's here!'

Following his gaze, she saw Rod and Christina with some students at the end of the corridor they were in. They were obviously going into one of the display halls, which she and Jamie had recently left.

Even from a distance it was easy to see that the Italian girl was sophisticated and self-assured. It was something to do with the way she moved. Allie felt herself flushing as she realised that Rod had obviously preferred the company of the other woman to herself. Well, who could blame him after the way she'd behaved? He probably thought she was a gauche schoolgirl. He'd never be interested in her when there were women like Christina in the world.

Trying to tell herself it didn't matter, she turned back to Jamie. 'He told me he was helping her with a student problem. It doesn't seem much of a problem to me. They're enjoying a day out.'

Jamie looked at her and grinned. 'You sound a bit miffed. Surely you don't fancy him yourself.'

She gave him a playful punch on the arm. 'Don't be ridiculous!' She remembered what Sarah had said, and realised that two people now suspected that she liked Rod a bit too much for her own good. 'I just don't appreciate being let down and brushed aside for someone else,' she added.

'I know it might look that way, but to be fair, I expect she needed another staff member to help with the visit and probably no one wanted to go with her. He's a good bloke, and obviously his duty is to the school, so don't feel too badly about it. I'm sure it wasn't a case of choosing to go with the art class instead of you.'

She raised her eyebrows. 'Really?'

'Well — she might be a good looker, but she's not popular. I wouldn't put it beyond her to manoeuvre Rod into this situation. He can hardly refuse to help with her students.'

'You're very perceptive,' she teased. 'Almost like a woman.'

Jamie put his arm lightly around her. 'In any case, you've got me — so what are you complaining about?'

'You're absolutely right.' She smiled brightly at him. 'What more could a girl want?' And suddenly, she didn't want to see the other group. Being on such poor terms with her boss, a day away from him was just what she needed. 'Let's keep our distance from them! After all, this is our day off.'

'Suits me. They'll only be here for the morning anyway on a half-day visit. But this place is so big it would be difficult to find them again.'

*　*　*

Later, when Allie's mind was saturated with all she'd seen, they had a quick lunch high on the gallery terrace. 'I can't take any more in,' she said ruefully. 'I think I need to come back and look at it all more slowly. I've seen so many wonderful things that my head is reeling.' She was silent for a moment, just looking around at the spectacular views, and let her gaze linger on the huge dome of the Cathedral which was now almost on a level with them. 'Florence is so beautiful. It's completely overwhelming.'

'You'll get used to it — but I remember how bowled over I was when I first arrived.' Jamie's face was serious for a moment. 'Now I just take it for granted, I suppose — but it's a pretty amazing place.'

Stifling a yawn, Allie grinned apologetically.

'What you need is some good fresh air. I was going to take you to the Pont Vecchio but everywhere is so busy that I vote we go to the Boboli Gardens instead. You can see the Pitti Palace there too, though we probably won't go inside today.'

The weather was perfect for the gardens, warm and sunny.

'If I said this was a beautiful place, the description wouldn't do it justice.' Allie's face shone with delight as she turned to Jamie. 'There is just so much of it. The Neptune Fountain is amazing, the views over Florence are truly wonderful, and there's some sort of magic in this lovely pure air.'

They laughed together at the Bacchus Fountain. 'I know from the guide books that he was the god of wine in Roman times, but what a strange little man!' Allie commented.

'Yes — he was a dwarf.' Jamie took her arm. 'There's so much more of Florence that I'd like to show you, so we must come again.'

He looked so eager that she wondered if he was falling for her. He was a good friend, but did she want anything more from him?

The thought of Rod came into her mind, which was just stupid. The trouble was that, in comparison, Jamie still seemed to be very much a boy. Then she shook the thoughts away; she was here to work, not find a man.

It was all part of being a woman, this inability to keep life in separate compartments, she thought. So, gently squeezing his hand, she said, 'That would be great!' Then she couldn't resist adding, 'We must ask Sarah to come another time — that would be fun.'

She tried to gauge his reaction. He

didn't look embarrassed, just said, 'Well
— if you'd like to, but I think It's great
just the two of us. Anyway my
motorbike won't take three.' He looked
satisfied with this excuse.

'How about Liz and Pete? They
offered me a lift in their car. We could
all come and make a party of it.'

'Hmm,' was all he said and the
subject was dropped.

★ ★ ★

When they returned, Rod caught her
on her way upstairs to her room. It was
almost as though he was waiting for
her.

'Allie.' He appeared slightly uncomfortable as he addressed her.

She raised her eyebrows inquiringly.
After seeing him with the Italian
woman earlier in the day, she was
determined not to be too friendly.

'Yes?' Her tone was brisk.

'Er — ' Yes, he was definitely
uncomfortable. 'In response to your last

125

statement which, as you know, I passed on to the police, some officers called here this afternoon.'

Her heart sank and she grasped the smooth wood of the banister rail. 'Did — did they want to speak to me again?' Her mind began to race, wondering if they were furious with her for not telling them everything in the first place. Or, worse, were they suspicious?

'Yes, they did — but mainly they wanted to search your room.' He looked directly at her as though daring her to query what he was saying.

'My room?' She clung to the rail with shaking hands, as it seemed to be the only thing that was keeping her upright.

'And of course, I wasn't here. So will they come back?' It was a nightmare, a terrible dream where she couldn't wake up. 'Why do they want to go into my room? Don't they believe me? Do they think I've got something hidden in there?'

She could hear her voice rising and the words tumbling out and almost falling over themselves. 'Why, Rod, why?' She tried to read his face but found nothing of comfort there. Her hands were clammy and she risked letting go of the banister to wipe one on her trousers.

'They . . . er . . . won't come back.'

Why was he hesitating? His speech was always so positive. It struck her that it was the second time she'd heard him say 'er' in the last few minutes.

'Thank goodness! They won't be back.' The relief was like a velvet blanket thrown over her mind. Then, in her usual cheeky matter, she said, 'So did you vouch for me and tell them you thought I was innocent of absolutely everything?'

'No — they won't be back because they've already checked your room.'

Staggering slightly, she thought how ridiculous it was to have this conversation halfway up the stairs. And then what he'd said really hit her, and she gasped out loud.

He put out a hand to steady her and

she shook him off angrily. 'You let them search my room, go through my things when I wasn't here!' She said the words slowly, trying to take in the significance of it all.

'I'm sorry. I know you're upset but . . .'

'Upset?' she shrieked. 'I'm more than upset. I can't believe you let that happen. It's disgusting. What kind of person are you? What kind of place are you running here?' Her hand was running through her hair and she was close to tears. Tears of rage and hurt, and somehow of feeling let down.

'Come into my office. You're shouting.'

'No, I won't — and I don't care if everyone hears what you've done. It's disgusting!' she cried again. 'I'm going home now. I'm going home.' She could feel the tears on her face.

He mustn't have the satisfaction of seeing her cry. She turned quickly and fled up the rest of the stairs and along the corridor to her door. But when she opened it, she realised that he was behind her — and try as she might, she couldn't push him out of the way.

'You're becoming hysterical.' He grabbed her elbows and propelled her into the room, then followed.

'Get out! Get out!' she yelled — and then suddenly the anger left her and there was only fear left. 'What are they going to do to me?'

'Nothing, believe me.'

She looked up at him. 'Nothing?'

'No, absolutely nothing. It was just a check because you were on a certain plane. It wasn't personal and I'm truly sorry, but there was nothing I could do to stop them.' He grinned half-heartedly. 'I might have a degree of influence here — but as regards the Italian law, I was powerless to intervene.'

'No. I suppose not.'

While he'd been talking, he'd somehow taken her into his arms. Now she realised her head was on his shoulder and his white shirt was damp with her tears. An extraordinary thought entered her mind as to how broad and comforting his shoulder was, and how cool the crispness of his shirt felt against her hot face.

'It's over now, and I don't think they'll want to see you again.'

She looked wildly round the room. 'But my things! They've touched all my things.' She shuddered. 'They've probably been through everything and it's horrible — horrible.'

'If it's any consolation, there was a woman police officer with them and I'm sure it would have been her, so try not to worry so much.'

'It doesn't make any difference. I'm still going home. There's no way I could stay here now.' Her voice broke. 'I should never have come. Everything has gone wrong.'

'I really don't want you to leave.'

'You don't?' She looked up at him in astonishment.

'Of course not — and in any case, it wouldn't be a good idea if you suddenly left for home now.'

'Why on earth not? You can't tell me

what to do.' She knew it sounded schoolgirlish but suddenly she was full of resentment again.

'I want you to stay — and besides, just think. It would look very bad if you left now. Far better to sit it out.'

Her mind grappled with the problem of whether he wanted her to stay for himself or to avoid any more bad publicity for the school. Then her body wilted in his arms, suddenly overcome with exhaustion.

Leading her to the bed, Rod sat her gently down.

'Have a rest and then you'll probably feel a lot better.' He crouched down in front of her. 'I'm sorry about today but something cropped up.'

'Yes, we saw you at the Uffizi Gallery with Christina this morning.'

'I wasn't out with Christina, as such, but helping with a scheduled student trip.' His brows drew together. 'You said 'we'. Who were you with?'

'Does it matter?'

'Of course it does. You must be

careful, Allie. You've already had one strange encounter and I'm responsible for you. So who were you with? Surely you haven't had the opportunity to meet anyone since you arrived.'

She could tell by his voice that he was definitely not pleased. It made her feel as though now she had the upper hand of the situation.

It was a great temptation not to tell him, and then she realised how stupid that would seem. 'If you must know, it was Jamie. I thought you knew anyway.' She gave him a bright smile. 'He's a nice, uncomplicated guy and I like his company.' And if he got the impression that she was less than delighted with his, that was okay with her.

'Right,' he said slowly, standing up, and she felt he had mentally withdrawn from her. 'I'll leave you now — but you know where I am if you want to talk any more about it all.'

'Yes, okay,' she said without looking at him and after a moment she heard the door close softly behind him.

8

Weary and frighened, Allie sank further into the bed feeling drained of all energy. Glancing around her, she thought everything looked just the same, with not a thing out of place. In fact, if she hadn't been told that the room had been searched, she wouldn't have known.

Her breath came out in a big sigh as she wondered where the happy, high-spirited girl she used to be had gone. Surely the police must know that she was completely innocent because nothing had been found.

Desperately she twisted her hands together. The mere thought that some-one had touched her things, her most intimate things, made her feel physically sick. But Rod had assured her it had been a woman who had performed the search; was it really so bad? Her first reaction had been to catch the next plane home. However, thinking it through, it was obvious that if she left now it would look as though she was guilty in some way — or at the very least questionable.

The best thing to do was put it from her mind and carry on with her job. Also, she admitted, Rod was right — there was nothing he could have done where the police were concerned. He couldn't have stopped the search happening and her behaviour towards him now made her cringe with embarrassment. It must have been the effect of shock, but that was no excuse and she'd better get herself together and apologise.

Sliding from the bed, she decided to go to his office right away, then found that her legs were too shaky to go down the stairs. Maybe later would be better, when she'd got over the shock, for it would be awful if she burst into tears in front of him. If only she wasn't such a mess! It was dreadful to know that just her being here had caused the school so much trouble; it was a wonder Rod didn't send her home himself.

Finally, filling her head with what she hoped were positive thoughts she made her way his office. *Why is it*, she wondered, *that I always feel like a naughty schoolgirl as I knock on his door?*

'Allie!' He looked up as she entered and, amazingly, he was smiling. 'How are you feeling now?' He got up from his desk and took her arm, leading her to a chair.

'Rod,' she said firmly, 'I'm sorry. I behaved very badly earlier on.' Her voice wobbled. 'It was the shock, I think — the thought that someone had been through my things.'

'It's all right.' He didn't return to his chair but stood beside her. 'You don't have to apologise. Anyone would have reacted the same way.'

'Thanks for understanding.' She tried not to show how relieved she felt.

Abruptly changing the subject, as

though it was of no significance, he said softly, 'Do you fancy coming to Lucca tomorrow?'

'Lucca?' She could feel herself grinning in delight. 'But — ' her face fell — 'I'm meant to be working tomorrow.'

'Yes, but I've got to collect something there and you need to get out of here for a day. We'll call it an educational visit.' His smile filled his eyes and was so infectious that she gave a small giggle.

'Educational visit,' she said. 'I can live with that.' Then with a flash of impishness, she added, 'In that case I feel I should be wearing a gymslip.'

At that she caught an expression in his eyes that made her blush.

'That's it, then — we'll go tomorrow. Dress optional.'

She went back to her room smiling.

★　★　★

The next day it was another morning full of promise, with a slight haze on the distant hills that she now knew meant it would be a lovely day. Dressing casually in white trousers and sleeveless black top, she firmly placed at the back of her mind her fears of the day before. Full of excitement, she ran downstairs to meet Rod outside the school.

Already standing at the passenger door of his car, he was casually dressed in cotton trousers and a short-sleeved shirt. He was also smiling at her, and her spirits lifted further.

'We'll drive to Florence station and catch the train.' Without waiting for a reply he continued, 'You haven't travelled on one yet and Italian trains are comfortable, clean and run on time. You'll enjoy the experience.' Opening the passenger door, he saw her into the car.

Sitting beside him she was aware of his nearness, and as he brushed against her she noticed the strength in his hard, muscled arm. All at once, realising that they were out of their usual business environment, Allie felt unusually shy.

Licking her dry lips, she knew this outing was strictly pleasure, intimate — and perhaps dangerous to her peace of mind.

'You look very nice,' he said, glancing across at her and as she looked up and met his eyes, she saw they were full of appreciation. She looked down at her crisp white trousers contrasting with the black top. 'Thank you,' she said demurely. 'I forgot my gymslip needed pressing.'

He laughed out loud, and the car was a vehicle full of fun and laughter as they drove to the station.

★ ★ ★

The journey, as he promised, was quick and the train comfortable and clean. Once there, Rod pulled a map from his pocket and studied it, which gave her the opportunity to watch his face, and think that this day could be important. If only they could manage a whole day together without quarrelling, she resolved to do her best to stay on friendly terms.

Entering the walled city, she was startled when he took her hand and went on to say casually, 'The great composer Puccinni was born here. We'll take a look at his house after lunch.' This was a different man from the one at school, and staying on friendly terms was going to be easy at this rate.

Was it the mention of Puccinni or the touch of his hand that suddenly made her think she could hear distant music? Deciding she was thinking like a lovesick teenager, she made an effort to concentrate on her surroundings. 'I'd love to walk around the top,' she said wistfully, glancing back over her shoulder at the red brick wall.

'Another time maybe.' He squeezed her fingers.

Still holding hands, they strolled the narrow streets to look at the Cathedral as it nestled against the Campinile. 'What was the Campinile built for?' she asked him.

'Just a lookout tower originally,' he answered. 'I know a nice little place in the main square where we can have lunch.'

During their meal she missed the touch of his hand, although she felt his eyes were sending her messages — or was it just the angle of the sun? After their meal he left her for half an hour to drink her coffee while he collected something nearby.

Sitting sipping the strong liquid, she admitted to herself that she couldn't wait for him to come back. She would have to take herself in hand. This was not why she'd come to Italy — and surely the boss was off limits.

'All done.' She jumped as he placed his hands on her shoulders. Turning to look up at him, at that moment, the knowledge that he was off limits was particularly hard to remember.

'Let's go and see the house where Puccini was born.' He pulled her lightly to her feet, keeping one hand clasped in his own.

It was a happy and rather drowsy girl who, later, waited for the train back to Florence. 'Thank you Rod, for bringing me here. It's been a lovely day.'

'You deserved a treat.'

'I did?' Her voice rose with surprise.

'Yes, I know how hard you're working at the language and now you're also beginning to use it. I'm pleased with you.'

'I only use it when I'm sure I'm not going to get out of my depth. I wouldn't want to make a fool of myself because not many of the others know about my problem with Italian.'

The words were said lightly but her heart was bouncing around. Rod was pleased with her — what more could she want?

'You've also had a difficult time with the police and one thing and another. I thought it would be good for you to get away for a day.'

It almost sounded as though he cared about her. *This won't do*, she thought as the train neared Florence. *What's*

141

happening to me? Italy is turning me into a lovestruck teenager. She shook away the thought.

★   ★   ★

Arriving back at Florence, she couldn't help turning to him with a grin. 'I feel as though I've played truant from school for the day.'

'Surely that's not what you used to do,' he teased. 'But we're going to continue with our truancy.'

'We are?' Her eyes were flashing with mischief. 'And just what are we going to do now?'

'We're going to finish the day by having dinner here.'

'Brilliant,' she breathed. 'What a lovely ending to the day.'

'We'll leave the car and walk. There's a little place I know that's not very far from here.'

He knew a lot of nice little places to eat. Perhaps his social life was more full than she thought? But she was determined to enjoy the moment.

Once settled in the small, intimate restaurant, she almost forgot she was with her boss and told Rod more about her life at home and the trouble she had experienced with her car at the last school where she taught.

'So I was usually late,' she finished. 'Not exactly an ideal teacher. Quite a bad example for the children, really.'

To her relief, he laughed. 'I notice this sort of thing didn't come out in your interview.'

'No.' She giggled. 'I was very careful what I said.'

'At least, living on the premises here, you won't have that problem so I'd better forget that you told me.' He definitely saw the funny side of her problems and was smiling across at her during their dinner.

'I love pasta,' she sighed as she finished her meal. 'Sometimes I think it was the main reason I wanted to come to Italy.' He was smiling again and she couldn't believe how relaxed they were in each other's company. This day was turning more and more into a date between two people who were attracted to each other, and less and less like a member of staff being taken out by the head teacher.

As they made their way back to the car, she resolved not to think about it until she was alone in her room. For the moment she would just enjoy the lovely relationship they'd built up during the day.

He was holding her hand again, as he'd been doing most of the day, which both delighted and also confused her. They weren't speaking but just enjoying being together when something occurred to jolt her from her beautiful dreamlike state.

As they approached Rod's car, they passed a row of motorbikes and scooters. Nothing unusual in that, for Florence was full of motorbikes. They were parked along most of the roads but something caught her attention and a thought at the back of her mind disturbed her. She shook her head trying to clear it. Then her step faltered and she almost stopped.

'What's the matter?' He looked down at her with concern. 'Did you twist your ankle or something?'

Suddenly her mouth was too dry to even answer him, for a dark figure was approaching one of the bikes. There was something familiar about him — something that made her shiver and want to look away. But she kept on looking, then wished she hadn't — for as the figure turned his head, she recognised him as the sinister man from the airport.

'Allie?' Rod stopped. 'Whatever is the matter? You're squeezing my hand as though you're afraid of falling.'

The fact that they'd stopped so abruptly attracted the attention of the dark figure and he looked straight at her. In his face she could see the recognition that was mirrored in her own, and she gasped out loud. Then the man's eyes took in Rod beside her, turned swiftly away and was astride his bike and revving the engine.

'Let's get into the car.' Her voice shook and she was aware of feeling cold. 'Please, Rod — quickly, let's get out of here.'

No sooner had she spoken than she was settled in the passenger seat and they were driving in the direction of the school.

'Tell me what's upset you.' He made to pull in at the side of the road.

'Don't stop, please don't stop! I just want to get back. That figure who was getting on his motorbike — it was the same man, Rod! The same man I saw at the airport.'

'You recognised him? Are you absolutely sure?'

'Yes.' She realised her hands were linked together so tightly that the feeling was going from her fingers. She started to massage them back to life without being aware of what she was doing.

'Yes — there's no mistaking him even

in the fading light. And he saw me.' Realising she was on the verge of tears, she swallowed and went on more firmly, 'I just know he recognised me, and when he saw you he turned away.'

Rod looked bewildered. 'What is it about him that scares you so much? He was surely just someone you noticed while you were waiting.'

'I just don't know. I suppose it seems stupid, but there was something about him that I can't forget. I feel instinctively that he was up to no good and I would hate to meet him again.'

'In that case I'm very glad you eventually reported it to the police. And you really think he recognised you?' Rod asked quietly.

'He must have done. He looked straight at me.' Overcome with sudden panic, Allie twisted around to look through the back window. There were several cars following them, and she sighed with relief. Then, in between two of the cars, she glimpsed a motorbike.

'There's a motorbike following us!'

She made to grab his arm and remembered just in time that he was driving. 'Do you think it's him? Is he following us?'

For a moment he touched her hand. 'Allie, Florence — in fact, all of Italy — is full of motorbikes both large and small. It would be very unusual for one not to be behind us.'

Her heart rate seemed to slow at his calming words and she managed the rest of the journey by breathing deeply and trying to unwind. He must think that she was just a hysterical female, and she wasn't. She was a happy-go-lucky kind of girl usually, but there was something going on here that she couldn't handle. The relief as they drew into the school car park was incredible and instantly she felt safe — just like being at home.

Her fright over, she turned impulsively to Rod.

'Thank you very much for a lovely day.' Without even thinking about it, she leaned across and kissed him on the cheek.

The kiss was just one of affection but as she started to draw away, she found herself being pulled into his arms and kissed thoroughly on the lips. It happened so quickly that she was in his arms before realising it. A glorious mixture of feelings flooded through her. All the anxiety left her — in fact, all her power of thought evaporated. Now there was only delicious sensation and the most wonderful excitement dancing through her body.

Those arms were warm and safe and, resting against him, she wanted to stay there and never pull away while his questing lips triggered magical sensations she had never experienced before.

Then the lights of another car swung into the car park. With great reluctance, Rod released her. Not waiting for him, Allie opened her door, said 'Goodnight' in a shaky little voice that sounded most unlike hers, and rushed into the school.

9

After a restless night, striving vainly to get her thoughts in some sort of order, Allie skipped breakfast and made her way to the courtyard. Standing once more at her favourite fountain, she watched the droplets of water, caught in the rays of a weak sun, disappearing just like her daydreams. Looking out over the panorama of slopes and olive trees, with a cloak of mist lying above the hills, she was overwhelmed, as usual, with the beauty of the place. Even her jumbled thoughts dropped to the back of her mind as the atmosphere calmed her.

Since the events of yesterday, she really couldn't make out how Rod felt about her. It certainly hadn't been a day out with the boss; they'd been two people getting to know one another, enjoying each other's company.

Whatever happened, she resolved, she mustn't fall in love with him. At one point it would have been the last thing on her mind — but now it would be so very easy.

Turning, she was suddenly aware of not being alone and her breath caught — for Christina was right beside her, looking both immaculate and beautiful. She was the last person she wanted to see — and besides, the woman had no right to look so good first thing in the morning.

'The police were here,' she stated without even saying good morning. 'I saw them go to your room the day before yesterday.'

'Really?' Allie forced her voice to sound cool and even. She wasn't in the mood for the Italian woman's frostiness this morning and hoped she'd go away. But somehow she knew there was more to come, and mentally braced herself for what followed.

'It will give the school a bad reputation if the police keep coming here.'

The spite in the woman's voice was something she could almost touch.

'Really,' she said again and turned back to the fountain, hanging on to her self-control. But inside, her temper rose at the deliberate unkindness being directed at her.

Christina moved round to stand at her shoulder. 'No wonder Rod took you out yesterday. Best thing he could have done, getting you away from the school so that things could settle down.' She looked directly, scornfully, at the younger girl. 'Of course, you know we are an item. I think that is the English term for it. So don't get any ideas, little new girl.'

Allie's eyes flashed and she tossed her head but her voice was cool.

'I congratulate you on your very good English, but tell me — are you naturally rude and unkind, or do you have to work at it?'

She forced herself to walk away slowly and deliberately. But once out of sight, she quickened her step. Inside she was shaking.

Eventually, feeling calmer, she went over the brief conversation in her mind. Was it true that Rod only took her out to get her away from the school? Maybe he didn't want her talking about what had happened. But he'd only had to ask her to keep quiet about it. He hadn't needed to hold her hand, to laugh with her, or then kiss her in a way that touched her soul.

Resolutely she squared her shoulders and put the conversation with Christina from her mind. What she needed was another serious talk with Jan. Tonight she would phone and bring her friend up to date about everything. She'd also better programme these phone calls into her budget.

★   ★   ★

'Where did you get to yesterday?' Sarah teased her at coffee break.

'Lucca.' Allie grinned broadly. 'And it was great.'

'You went with Rod?' Jamie's voice

had an edge to it.

Oh, dear — she wasn't an unkind girl, but she'd forgotten all about Jamie and the idea that he might be keen on her.

'He thought I should know more about the area,' she said gently, 'and was nice enough to take me — just like you did when we went to Florence. You are all so very kind here.' Then she brightened and continued, 'You two should go, if you haven't been before. It's well worth a visit.'

Sarah turned to Jamie eagerly. 'Why don't we go there for a change?'

'Yeah, why not?' His gaze shifted to her. 'Saturday — we'll go Saturday. Obviously Allie won't want to come with us as she's already been.' Putting down his empty cup, he said abruptly, 'Well, I'm off back to class.'

She knew he was hurt — but if only he would realise it, he and Sarah were absolutely perfect for each other.

After they had watched Jamie disappear inside, Allie turned to Sarah.

'You do like him — don't you? In spite of everything you said to me.'

Sarah returned her grin. 'Yes, I think he's great and we were getting on so well before you arrived — but, well . . . you know . . . when I thought he was keen on you, I decided to just take a back seat.'

'You're a star, and a very lovely person. But honestly, I just think of him as a friend, so don't worry about me.'

'Yes — I can guess exactly where you're heading with the dishy Rod.'

'Don't talk about it. I've already been warned off this morning by the lovely Christina.' Allie took a moment to relive the encounter. 'You know, she was almost vindictive.'

'Take no notice of her. She's a nasty piece of work and none of us really think he likes her that much. It's all on her side. So you go for it and good luck.' She chuckled. 'Especially if it keeps you away from Jamie!'

'Hint taken!' Allie laughed back as

she closed the door behind her.

'Allie!' It was Liz, calling her through the open door of her classroom. 'The students will be here in a moment so just a quick word, but Pete and I wondered if you'd like a lift into Florence on Saturday?'

Allie thought quickly. 'Yes, please — I'd love the opportunity to wander around. I want to explore the Ponte Vecchio Bridge with its little shops. It looks so quaint.'

'Good. We're driving in early morning. Then we'll split up, meet you somewhere for coffee at some point during the afternoon, and bring you back. Will that be okay for you?'

'That's perfect, Liz — just perfect. Thanks very much.' A day on her own was something she could do with, she reflected. It would be good to be away from the school and simply wander around Florence with just her camera. And she quickened her step, with all thoughts of Christina and Rod pushed from her mind.

Early on Saturday, dressed in sandals with a cotton skirt and toning top, Allie was ready and waiting for her friends outside the school.

'We'll drop you at the Ponte Vecchio,' said Peter. 'I expect you want to explore it — most people do.'

'You must have read my mind.' She laughed. 'Am I so predictable?'

Driving along beside the River Arno, Liz pointed to a cafe. 'That's where we'll pick you up this afternoon, around half past four. If we're not there on time just sit outside with a coffee and wait, but we'll definitely be there.'

'That's great.' As she looked through the window at the cafe, she noticed the usual row of motorbikes and scooters along the side of the road. For a moment she felt a twinge of panic. *No, don't be silly*, she told herself. The man from the airport surely wouldn't be in Florence today — and she wasn't likely to ever see him again.

Once out of the car, she concentrated on what was going on around her and deciding to leave her discovery of the Ponte Vecchio Bridge for a while longer, sauntered along beside the Arno.

Usually a girl who loved company, Allie found she was enjoying her own space. There was time to think without the routine of the school intruding. Florence was full of people but, like her, they were all doing their own thing. No one was interested in her and it gave her a wonderful feeling of freedom.

Stopping to gaze across the water, she folded her arms on the wall and thought about the subject that was always on her mind lately — Rod. Once again she wondered why he'd taken her to Lucca. Was it to get her away from the school, as Christina suggested — or was it, as she hoped, to give her a welcome day out and enjoy some time together?

Last night when she'd phoned her friend, Jan had advised her to sit tight and see what happened while, if possible, keeping out of Christina's way.

'It sounds very much to me as if she's jealous,' Jan mused.

'If only . . . But she's lovely, Jan. He couldn't possibly prefer me to her. She's very sophisticated and sort of — *female*. Well — I suppose sexy is the word I'm looking for, if you know what I mean.'

Jan had laughed. 'Perhaps he likes his women young and lively, like you — the type that attracts trouble.'

'Thanks! You're doing wonders for my self esteem. But honestly, do you think I should offer to resign?'

'No, of course not. As I say, just sit tight and enjoy Italy. It's where you always wanted to go. You'd be mad to come back so soon.'

Her mind was easier after their conversation, but there was a lot she hadn't told Jan about — such as the visits from the police and the sinister man on the motorcycle.

She gave herself a shake. It was really

silly, wasting a perfectly good day in Florence mulling over her problems.

Making her way along the river to the Garibaldi Monument, she crossed over the road and strolled along, past the cafes and shops. It was this side of the road where all the bikes were parked. *Does everyone use this form of transport in Italy?* she thought as she watched hordes of young people either parking their bikes or driving off again. The idea flashed into her mind that maybe she should get a scooter if she was here long enough. It would be cheaper to run than a car.

She was still thinking about whether or not she'd like a scooter herself when she saw the man from the airport again.

This time he was parking his bike. Allie stopped absolutely still, trying to tell herself that it wasn't him. But there was that certain something about him that she recognised. Then, realising he might see her, she dodged quickly into a shop. Logically there was no reason why she should hide from him; only a sixth sense that caused her to feel threatened.

Aware of her quickened heartbeat and dry mouth, she noted with relief that the shop sold odd gifts aimed at tourists and also postcards. Turning her back on the shop entrance, she rifled through the rack of cards, taking a long time and choosing several. After all, an extra postcard to family and friends would be appreciated. Taking as long as possible over her choice, she then managed to buy stamps from the same place and at last had no longer any excuse to linger.

Slowly and methodically she placed the items in her shoulder bag, but her mind was racing. Somehow she had to see that the man was handed over to the police, but how could she manage it? Should she telephone them? She had no idea what to do but, once outside, she could contact the school and speak to Rod. He'd know the best way to handle it. Her shoulders slumped slightly with relief at that comforting thought.

In the meantime she could get the details of his bike! Before, when she'd seen him, it had all happened too quickly — but this time, she knew exactly where it was parked, and he had walked off purposefully in the direction of the square. Rummaging in her bag for a pen and piece of paper, she had a flash of inspiration. There, at the bottom, were her small digital camera and a pair of sunglasses.

Quickly she put on the glasses and before she could change her mind, left the shop. Anxiously she peered around, but there was no sign of the man. Her heart was beating rapidly and her fingers were so damp that she had to rub them on the sides of her skirt before she could line up the camera and take her shots. Pushing up her glasses she took several pictures in quick succession.

Now feeling more confident, instead of leaving immediately, she hesitated to put away her camera and was just in the process of zipping her bag when something attracted her attention. The man she now feared was coming back towards his bike.

Hastily she swung round, pushed her glasses in place and crossed the road with a group of people.

There was no way of knowing whether he'd seen her, and her legs were now heavy with fear as she forced herself not to look round. The group were moving towards the Ponte Vecchio Bridge and it was like a lifeline, for there were so many people, milling around or gazing into shop windows, that she could easily be lost in the throng.

As she moved forward with the others, her step faltered and a question again flashed into her mind. Why exactly was she frightened? It was something she hadn't thought about sensibly, for she'd always panicked when she saw the motorbike and rider. But why? It was a question she'd never asked herself. Probably it was due to his odd behaviour when she first arrived and all jumbled up with her worry at being left at the airport with no one to meet her. Surely she didn't need to be in this state. What could he do to her? She hadn't witnessed a crime or anything. She slowed her step, took off her glasses and tried some deep breaths.

She was enchanted with the medieval bridge and the jumble of shops along both sides, some actually overhanging the river. But there was nothing jumbled about the objects for sale in the shops, which were classy and full of both antique and new jewellery. This was a place she'd always wanted to visit, and she forced herself to behave like a normal tourist. Now calmer, she decided she would phone Rod anyway — just to let him know that the sinister man was around.

It seemed only seconds before she was speaking to him.

'Where exactly are you?' She could hear an uneasy edge to his voice.

At her answer, he said, 'Good girl, you're among plenty of people. What part of the bridge are you on?'

She quickly lifted her head and glanced in front of her. 'Nearer the beginning than the end. Oh, I don't know. Probably towards the middle. There's such a crowd of people, it's hard to say.' She went on quickly before he could reply. 'But I've been thinking, there's no reason he would hurt me. I haven't witnessed him committing a crime or anything. There's no cause for me to be scared, but I know the police will want to know where he is.' She knew she was babbling but couldn't stop. 'I've taken pictures of his bike with my camera so I've got all the details.' She was pleased with herself and was sure he'd be impressed.

He didn't answer immediately and then said slowly. 'Did he see you?'

'Oh, I don't think so, although he came back just as I was finishing.'

'What?' The sound exploded into her ear. 'Stay where you are! Don't leave the bridge. I'm coming to get you.'

'You are?' She gasped.

'If you see him, go into one of the shops and stay there. Pretend to be wanting to buy something.'

'But they're mostly jewellers — and you should see the prices. I wouldn't last five minutes in a shop like that.'

'You've got an advantage,' he said. 'You're English. Pretend you don't understand them and you should be able to draw it out.'

'But . . . ' she protested.

'Allie — shut up. We're wasting time. Just stay there and go into a shop if you see him. Don't worry — I'll look in every one of them until I find you.'

And he rang off.

For a moment she savoured the words, 'until I find you.' It sounded so romantic. But she'd better do as she was told. There had been something in his voice that brought back her feelings of unease.

10

Checking her watch, Allie wondered how long it would take Rod to reach her. The crowds on the bridge were becoming thicker and she knew he would have a terrible job finding her. Now the over-riding problem was what she could do until he came. There may be masses of people, but she was still very exposed. She just wanted somewhere to hide. Surely that wasn't asking too much, but in this bustling spot there simply wasn't anywhere.

Perhaps she'd better do as he suggested and go into a shop. Without any more thought, she turned into the nearest one. This was a mistake, she knew immediately, looking at the quality of the jewellery. She should have checked in the window first. But she was here now, and it would be too embarrassing to run straight out again.

Smiling tentatively at the owner and feeling completely out of her depth, she licked her lips nervously while searching around vainly for the correct Italian phrase.

'You are perhaps English?'

'However did you know?' She laughed with a mixture of relief and surprise. The man appeared to be friendly. 'I thought with my dark hair and eyes I could pass for Italian.'

'It is the manner,' the man replied, 'and also the way you dress.'

Oh dear, she thought, her confidence draining away. *I wonder what he means by the way I dress. Surely I don't look frumpy.*

'Can I help you?'

She thought quickly. What would be the smallest, and perhaps the cheapest, item on sale? Then she had the answer. 'Yes — I'd like to see some earrings, please.'

'Gold or silver or — '

Surely silver would be cheaper. 'Oh — silver, please.'

When a selection was placed in front of her, Allie couldn't speak. Not usually a great lover of jewellery, she could well understand the appeal of the exquisite items displayed for her approval.

Picking up several pairs, she held each one in turn against her face and peered into the mirror. Anything to play for time. Knowing she was far from an expert where jewellery was concerned, she was completely out of her depth and it was a terrible strain. She'd never had any trouble making up her mind, and usually did everything as quickly as possible. Now she had to pretend to dither and be undecided in an effort to waste some time and, for her, it was verging on the impossible.

'I don't know,' she said at last. 'My boyfriend is buying them for me,' she improvised. 'I think perhaps he'd better come with me to make the final choice.' Then, starting to get into her role, she picked up two pairs at random and added, 'It will be a choice between these . . . ' Then she hesitated and picked up another pair. 'Or maybe these. Oh dear, I am sorry. I can't seem to make up my mind. They're all so beautiful.' Then, noting a faint look of impatience on the face of the man serving her, she said, 'Oh dear,' again. 'I will have to bring my boyfriend.' She placed the delicate silver items back on the velvet-covered tray. They were hardly something she could treat herself to as a holiday souvenir. The cost of them made her blink.

'Certainly — do bring him to help you decide.'

There was nothing else she could say. A sudden dizziness swept over her. Perhaps it was because the shop was warm and she was already hot and anxious and desperate to leave it and breathe some cool air. Lying didn't come at all easily to her, and she was uncomfortable.

'Grazie.' She murmured her thanks to the proprietor and emerged thankfully onto the bridge.

There was nothing for it but to repeat

the process in another shop. How she wished there was a corner where she could hide! But Rod had told her to go into the shops, and that's where he would look for her. Just entering them and pretending to buy sounded simple, but the nervous strain of playing a part was telling on Allie.

Each place she entered was a little area of safety, which she didn't want to leave. And then she struck lucky in one — for a friendly woman served her who was eager to know where she'd come from, and then began to tell her about her own travels.

Allie half listened, just happy to stay within the security of the shop and listen to the talkative woman. In fact, she wished she would keep talking forever so she could stay in the safety of the ancient premises.

She even called Allie over to the rear window so that she could admire the view of the river, pointing out the best position to stand.

Allie was charmed. 'May I take a

picture from here?'

The woman nodded. 'Of course.'

To pass more time Allie asked her about the history of the bridge, even though she had read about it before she left home. But it was easy to stay interested, as the woman was so enthusiastic about her subject. At one point she was even tempted to confide in her and ask if she could stay — but it all seemed too complicated. Then another customer entered, and the moment was gone. It was time to move on once more.

When she did eventually leave the woman's shop, she was surprised how much time had gone by. Surely Rod would be here soon? If not, she'd just have to repeat the shop process over again.

It was as she left the next place that she saw the man walking along towards her. Panic flooded through her and for a moment her limbs wouldn't respond. Then, somehow, she managed to turn on her heel and hurry swiftly along, hoping to lose herself amongst the other people.

Not knowing whether or not he'd seen her, she tried desperately not to run, which would draw attention to herself. So with head averted she walked swiftly, while all the time her mind ran in circles wondering what her next move ought to be. Should she dive into yet another shop — or was it better to keep on walking?

If only she hadn't come to the bridge! She could have sat in a cafe and waited for Rod, and felt safe with people at tables around her. Her trembling legs were heavy and she knew they would soon refuse to move. It was like one of those nightmares in which she wanted to run and couldn't move, or tried to scream and no sound came out when she opened her mouth. What should she do?

The decision was never made, for with a stab of terror she felt heavy hands land on her shoulders and she was swung round to face the man.

Completely incapable of movement, she stood frozen with fear. Forcing herself to look up, she saw that, close to, he was even more menacing.

Suddenly a sense of outrage filled her, outrage that she should be in such a position. It gave her the strength to struggle and kick out at him, but he simply dug his fingers into her shoulders until she thought she would cry out with pain.

Sliding his hands down her arms, he pulled her even closer and she felt his breath on her face. The sensation horrified her anew.

'Help . . . ' The sound of the word came out weakly, for her vocal cords were paralysed with terror.

No one appeared to hear. Then she remembered the Italian word for help and opened her mouth to yell, 'Aiuto,' but she only managed to say the first part of the word as the man clamped his huge hand across her mouth. The touch seemed revoltingly intimate and she wondered, idiotically, whether his hand was clean.

He put his mouth close to her ear. 'This is a warning, lady. Keep away from me and my bike. If you tell anyone about me, you'll regret it. If you set the police on me, my friends will also see that you regret it.'

His accent was hard to understand, but his meaning was all too clear.

He shoved her forward and the hands on her arms were no longer there.

Forcing herself to turn, she watched him disappear as though leaving the bridge. Why hadn't anyone come to her rescue? Then, looking around at the crowds, she realised that no one had noticed. There were several couples embracing; probably people had thought it was a lover's quarrel.

Stupidly, she'd been so frightened that she hadn't even noticed what he was wearing. What if she was asked to give a description of him? All at once she felt sick and shaky and moved close to a shop window. Reaction came swiftly and she rested her pounding head against the cool glass. Why did the man think that she was such a threat to him? There was obviously a great deal she didn't understand. She was terrified of him, and he appeared to feel threatened by her. But why? She had no idea. It was all a weird puzzle. If only Rod would hurry up and come — for dealing with that man was more than she could cope with.

Checking her watch she wondered how long she would have to wait. 'Rod . . . ' She actually formed the name, which came out as a whisper.

Then, just as if he'd heard her calling him, he was there. At last! Without thinking, she flung her arms around his neck. He was solid and secure and she knew now that she was safe.

'Allie — are you all right?' His voice was husky. 'I came as quickly as I could. I just dropped everything, and only stopped to telephone the police.' His arms were around her and he was holding her tightly. 'We've been working our way along the bridge, looking in every shop — and then I saw you standing here.'

Studying his face, she saw that his brows were drawn together with worry and his eyes were full of concern.

A movement caught her eye. She blinked in surprise, for beside him were two police officers.

'You've only just missed him,' she squeaked, thinking how absurdly high-pitched her voice sounded. 'He — he threatened me. But I think he's gone off the bridge now.'

The men stared at her. Rod held her away from him and said, in a low voice, 'Threatened you? What happened — are you sure you're all right? Did he hurt you? Because if he did . . . '

'No, no,' she interrupted. 'But tell them they're wasting time. Look . . . ' With shaking hands, she unzipped her bag, pulling out her camera and switching on the small screen. 'Look — that's his bike on the screen. It's parked along the road, on the opposite side.' She pushed the camera into the hands of the nearest officer. Rod spoke a few quick words to them and they turned and hurried back the way they'd come.

'Why is all this happening?' Her voice was muffled, as somehow she was in his arms again with her face pressed tightly against his chest. 'Oh, Rod — I'm so stupid. I can't even give a description of him. I was too frightened to take anything in.'

'You've been wonderful.' He hugged her tightly. 'I'm so proud of you. You've been so brave, and taking that photograph was a stroke of genius. Foolhardy and risky, but definitely a stroke of genius.'

'You think so?' Her eyes shone.

'Most definitely.' He grinned. 'Now, there's a lot to explain. I've been in contact with the police for several days. I'll tell you all about it, but not here. Do you want to go for a drink — perhaps some English sweet tea for shock?' He smiled. 'Or do you feel strong enough to head back to the school?'

She was quite happy where she was, in the comfort of his arms, and had no wish to go anywhere, but obviously they couldn't stay here. Already people were jostling them and trying to look past them into the shop window they were blocking.

'Let's go back.' She nearly said 'home', as the school seemed such a safe place after the events of this morning.

With his arm firmly around her, he walked her back to his car. There was one bad moment when they neared the spot where the motorbike had been parked, but it was missing and she gave a sigh of relief.

Having felt so alone and vulnerable looking in the jewellery shops, she was now safe and secure with Rod and it was a wonderful feeling. He telephoned Liz to tell her not to worry about bringing Allie back, and then fell silent, allowing her to sit quietly during the journey.

When they arrived back at the

school, he said gently, 'Come into my office. I'm sure you can do with something to drink now, and then you can tell me more about it.'

Soon she was sitting clutching a glass of wine and going over the whole episode, trying to remember every detail.

'But why did he threaten me? I just don't understand any of it. He always gave me a creepy feeling, but I was never really frightened before — not like I was on the bridge.' Covering her face with her hands, she realised it was all over, and tears of relief weren't far away.

'I don't think he was too worried at first. After all as far as you were concerned, he was just someone you saw when you arrived. He probably didn't think you were in Florence to stay anyway.'

Rod took a deep breath and continued. 'But when you took a picture of his bike, he must have seen you and realised you were on his trail. The picture was obviously something that could identify him to the police.' He hesitated. 'I know it was very brave of you, but really it was a risky thing to do. Didn't you stop and think?'

'I thought it was the right thing to do.' She heard a little strength coming back into her voice. 'Besides, he wasn't there at the time. I was unlucky that he came back when he did — but even so, I wasn't sure he'd actually seen what I was doing. And I was so pleased to have the picture, I suppose I didn't give it a lot of thought.'

'You were lucky he didn't try and take away your camera — but I suppose that really would have attracted attention, so he just decided to threaten you instead.' He took her hand and ran his thumb across her palm. 'You really have been incredibly lucky.'

'What will happen now?'

'As I said, I've been in contact with the police for the last few days, ever since you thought you saw him the day we went to Lucca. I dare say they'll follow him and try to pick up the rest of the gang. Actually, the police knew of him, but he's so far proved to be quite elusive. He could be a key member of a gang of thieves. There's nothing for you to worry about now. Obviously they will keep us informed.' He hesitated. 'He could even have popped something in your pocket to get it through customs and taken it out again when you think he pushed you, but there's not much point in worrying about that as I don't suppose we'll ever know.'

At last, she let her breath out in a big sigh of relief. *Nothing to worry about*. That sounded wonderful, and if the police picked up the rest of the gang, she could put his threat out of her mind.

Suddenly a picture of the man, with his threatening face close to her own, came rushing back in her mind and she realised she was totally exhausted. 'I must go up to my room, Rod. It sounds feeble, I know — but I'm so tired.'

'It's reaction. There's been a lot for

you to take in, coupled with the terrible experience you've had. A rest would do you good. But are you sure you'll be all right on your own? Is there anything you want?'

At that moment the phone rang and Allie took the opportunity to slide out, smiling her thanks and closing the door softly behind her.

* * *

Two hours later, a knock at the door woke her. Hoping, yet at the same time dreading it would be Red, she called out, 'Come in.'

Her breath caught as a person whom she was quite certain she didn't want to see glided into her room.

'Christina!' She propped herself up, feeling at a distinct disadvantage.

The Italian girl came close to the bed and glared down at her. For the second time that day, Allie felt threatened.

Christina spoke through clenched

teeth. 'You know Rod and I are more than colleagues. In fact . . . ' She left the sentence unfinished, leaving Allie to grasp her implication. 'And you're becoming a severe embarrassment to him and to the school.'

'What do you mean?' Allie swung her legs off the bed and stood up to face her rival. She was no longer tired; in fact, she was fired up with energy as her temper rose.

'I overheard him on the telephone to the police again. Don't you care about the reputation of the school? This school means everything to him.'

'None of this is my fault.' Allie's eyes flashed as she faced Christina, and her fists were tightly clenched, trying to keep control of her emotions. Goodness — a malicious thought entered her head — it was so tempting to slap her beautiful, contemptuous face.

'Of course you think he's paying you attention, but he's just trying to solve the situation. You mean nothing to him — nothing!' Christina practically spat out the last word, turned abruptly and left the room.

Once alone, Allie was so strung up that she thought she'd explode. Somehow she must let off steam, and she paced the room until she was calm enough to think.

This was definitely the end of her Italian dream. Looking back, she remembered how excited she'd been just a few days ago — and how pleased when Rod had been so nice about her language problems.

And now it was all over.

Letting herself slump onto the bed, she knew there was only one thing now she could do. It was to go home. There was dampness on her cheeks, and she brushed it away with her hand.

Later she'd ring Jan and check if there was a space in the flat where she could squeeze in for a time and then make her travel arrangements. But for now she would start packing. The physical activity was appealing.

She dragged her suitcase out and began collecting things from the wardrobe, flinging them down in a heap. Later she would fold them carefully — but for now, they could just pile up on the bed.

Suddenly, she stopped and dropped her head in her hands at the thought of going through all the worry of job-hunting again. For a moment she almost changed her mind — but she knew she couldn't stay here with Rod and Christina. She'd made a complete fool of herself already.

When there was a second knock on her door, she stormed over and flung it wide. It just had to be that woman again. 'I don't want you in my room!' she snapped through clenched teeth. There was a limit to what she could put up with, and today she'd reached it.

'Allie?' Rod looked puzzled. Then, looking beyond her into the room, he stalked in, slamming the door behind him. Striding over to the bed, he surveyed the untidy heap of clothes.

'What's going on?' He seemed genuinely at a loss.

'I'm leaving — that's what's going on!' Then, aware that she was shouting, she drew a deep breath and continued in a lower tone, 'I've just had a visit from your girlfriend, Christina — and frankly I've had enough.'

His expression hardened. 'She is not my girlfriend.' He said the words firmly and slowly. 'There is absolutely nothing between her and me, and there never will be.' He turned suddenly to face her, his eyes smouldering. 'How can you even think like this, after — ? I thought that we — '

'How can I believe you?'

'Listen to me.' He put his hands on her shoulders and shook her slightly. 'You bluffed your way through the interview, breezed into my school and turned my life upside down.' A smile spread across his face and lit up his eyes. 'I can't go back to the dull old ways now. You changed my life — it's as simple as that.'

He sounded serious, but a glance at his face revealed that he was still smiling and his eyes were full of warmth.

'I did?' she said softly, lifting her head to meet his gaze, yet hardly believing what she was hearing.

'Yes — and do you know what?' he gave an abrupt laugh. 'I love it. I simply can't go back to how things were before you came.'

As he spoke he was drawing her nearer to him and her heart was beating quickly. What was he saying? Did he want her here after all? Her thoughts were cut off as he added, 'So don't even think of going now.'

Then — like a dash of cold water in her face — he continued, 'Wait until the end of term.'

'Oh!' Her voice was small and she seemed to crumple. So he was quite happy to see her go — but at his convenience. The awful realisation came to her that Christina was right. Well, she wasn't standing for that.

Pulling away from his embrace, she straightened up, placed a hand on each hip and retorted, 'I'll go when it suits me — and it suits me now.' She added as an afterthought, 'I should have listened to Christina — but I just thought she was being bitchy.'

'Oh, no, you don't.' He caught each of her hands in his and dragged them up to clasp them against his chest. 'You were absolutely right about Christina — but you don't have to worry about her any more. Running an art class in the school hasn't worked out, and she's taking her class and joining another organisation.'

'But she didn't tell me anything about that.' Allie was genuinely puzzled.

'Don't let's bother about her. What I wanted to say was, wait until the end of term and we'll go together. Surely you didn't think I'd let you go on your own, do you?'

'Together?' She stared at him. 'Are you going back to live in England as well? You can't leave! It's your school

189

and you love it — I know you do. It's your life.' She paused for a moment and frowned. 'What do you mean exactly, 'we'll go together'?'

'Oh Allie, that's typical of you, jumping to conclusions. Of course I'm not giving up the school — but I must go back at the end of term to deal with one or two things. I expect you'll want to see your friends and family. And then we'll come back here together.'

She stared at him, wide-eyed. 'You mean you want me to come back, to continue working here?'

'Of course I do. What have I just been telling you?'

'Oh, Rod — I'd love to, I really would — but I'm worried I don't fit in.' She gave a slight grin. 'This term so far has been so disruptive, and I feel you must all be thoroughly fed up with me.'

He was drawing her towards him again. 'You're perfect. The students like you, and so do the staff. You've brought a breath of fresh air with your enthusiasm for Florence. Allie, you are an absolute asset.'

'I am?' Her mind was like cotton wool. This was awful; she seemed all of a sudden to have completely lost the ability to hold a proper conversation.

'Yes, my darling, you are. Everyone loves you — but more importantly, I love you and want you here with me. Please say you'll stay with me?' He smiled down at her. 'Apart from anything else, you need someone to look after you and stop you getting involved with strange men.'

He loved her! She knew that was what she'd been waiting to hear. He actually loved her, and she wanted to dance around the room.

Her voice returned then and, forcing herself to stand still, she murmured, 'Oh Rod — I'd like nothing better.'

'Think of the way it'll improve your Italian. Surely that's an incentive.' He was laughing at her. 'So will you stay?'

'Will I be able to give up my lessons?' she teased.

'You can have private ones with me,

if only you'll stay.'

'Yes, Rod — I'd love to.' Then an imp of mischief, a touch of the old Allie, took over as she added coyly, 'But only if you ask me to stay in Italian. After all, I'm here to learn the language.'

She listened, smiling, as his voice softly caressed her with the words. They were spoken slowly, and somehow she understood that it wasn't just the school that needed her. He finished in English. 'So, Allie Holt, will you come back with me?'

She took his face in her hands and looked deep into his eyes.

The Italian word for yes was very easy to say.

THE END

Other titles in the
Linford Romance Library:

JUST A MEMORY AWAY

Moyra Tarling

In hospital, Alison Montgomery cannot remember her own name. She hears the doctors' hushed whispers — sees their worried glances, which speak of the dark secrets lying just beyond the locked shutters of her memory. Then they bring her the stranger who says he's her husband. But why can't she remember loving a man as compelling as Nicholas Montgomery? And yet the shadows in his eyes clearly reveal that there's something in their past better left forgotten . . .